בס"ד

# Toba's Passage

### by Libby Herz
### illustrated by Dena Akerman

Hachai
PUBLISHING

# Toba's Passage

To my dear children Kehos, Sarah, Yehudis, and Tova.
May the light of Torah and mitzvos illuminate your lives. L. H.

First Edition 5776 / 2016

**Editor:** D.L. Rosenfeld
**Managing Editor:** Yossi Leverton
**Layout:** Moshe Cohen

ISBN: 978-1-935882-02-2
LCCN: 2016930382

**HACHAI PUBLISHING**
Brooklyn, N.Y.
Tel: 718-633-0100   Fax: 718-633-0103
www.hachai.com - info@hachai.com

Printed in China

# Table of Contents

Meet the Family ............................................................ 4

Chapter One   **The Letter** ...................................... 7

Chapter Two   **Saying Goodbye** .......................... 31

Chapter Three   **All Aboard!** ................................... 39

Chapter Four   **Lost**................................................. 55

Chapter Five   **America at Last!** .......................... 73

Chapter Six   **The Red-Headed Girl** ................. 85

Chapter Seven   **A New Life** ................................... 97

Chapter Eight   **Streets of Gold** .......................... 105

Chapter Nine   **Just Like Mama** ......................... 135

Chapter Ten   **The Search** ................................. 143

Chapter Eleven   **Found!** ....................................... 153

Chapter Twelve   **The Greatest Gift** ....................... 171

Historical Note ......................................................... 181

Glossary ................................................................... 187

# Meet the Family

**Toba** —  This brave eleven-year-old loves adventure. When she embarks on a journey across the ocean, she realizes just how much her family means to her.

**Velvel** —  Toba's clever nine-year-old brother always joins in her escapades. He has a head for numbers and is good at making new friends.

**Luba** —  Toba's three-year-old sister is absolutely adorable. Toba misses her terribly when the two are separated by the Atlantic Ocean.

**Mama** —  Mama is a strong, hard working woman who keeps the family going while her husband is far away in America.

**Papa —** Papa traveled to New York alone. He works from morning to night, trying to make enough money for tickets to bring his family to join him.

**Zeide —** Zeide is a bookbinder and a Torah scholar. Toba is very close to her Zeide and treasures the special siddur he gave her.

**Aunt Fronya —** Papa's sister is a cautious young woman who carries sadness with her. She worries about her *chosson* who disappeared after being drafted into the czar's army.

# Chapter One: The Letter

"Toba, catch!" My nine-year-old brother Velvel dashed into the water, saving our Shabbos tablecloth from floating across the Lavnes River.

"Wait for me!" I yelled, waving a long washing bat over my head. I was eleven years old, old enough to keep an eye on my little brother in the forest. The river was on the fringe of the shtetl, so we weren't *that* far from Mama. I shot into the water, following my brother, already knee deep in the icy river. I grabbed the drenched tablecloth and pulled it back to shore.

"Mama will be furious if we lose a Shabbos tablecloth," said Velvel. Thick white clouds puffed from Velvel's mouth as he spoke. "It took her half a year to embroider this one."

Velvel was right, too. In the past month, I had lost two headscarves, four handkerchiefs, and one old pair of pants to the Lavnes River. I wanted to show Mama that I was just as trustworthy as my little brother. And at the rate I was going, that would not be an easy feat.

Sometimes, I suspected that Mama had Velvel accompany me on laundry expeditions so that he could help me fetch lost items. I placed the tablecloth against a large rock. *Whack! Whack!* I swung the washing bat over my head and let it come down hard. I may not have been good at remembering things, but I was really good at hitting clothing with bats.

*Whack!*

"That ought to get the dirt out," I muttered under my breath.

I blew on my frozen hands before sticking them into the river with Luba's tiny dress. Birds chirped. A fat squirrel scurried up a nearby tree. The sound of hoof beats pierced the peaceful forest sounds. My breath caught in my throat. Thoughts of pogroms flashed through my mind. Mama had said we were safe from pogroms for now. But could someone be hiding in the forest in the middle of the day? A shiver ran up my spine. I ducked and grabbed Velvel down.

"Ouch, Toba, you're pinching me!" said Velvel.

"Shush!" I put my finger to my lips.

"Toba Czapelski!" A familiar voice boomed through the trees. The voice belonged to Zev Volf, our neighbor. We were safe. I brushed myself off, and pulled Velvel up.

"I can get up myself, Toba," Velvel brushed my hand away.

"Sorry, I was just trying to help," I said.

Zev jumped off his horse, straightened his enormous black yarmulka, and dusted his grey vest. His clothing was very old and had more holes than material. His vest looked like a pile of dry ashes were stitched together by a blind tailor. If only I had some material, I would make him a new one. It would be lovely.

"I have something for you," said Zev, "a letter to take to your Mama."

"A letter?" I asked. I dropped the washing bat to the floor. "For Mama?"

"Who is it from?" asked Velvel.

Zev didn't answer us. He thrust his arm into his leather satchel, and took out a thick, brown envelope.

"This letter," Zev Volf puffed out his chest, "traveled all the way across the Atlantic Ocean to Russia. Who is it from, you ask? Ah," Zev Volf laughed. "This, you will soon find out." He gave us a crooked smile.

I dropped the dress to the ground and dried my palms on my apron. I plucked the letter from Zev's hands. Velvel stood on his tiptoes. I stared at the large, loopy letters scrawled across the envelope.

"How many letters did Mama receive

this year?" asked Velvel.

"Maybe five or six," I said, bringing the letter to my nose. I loved the smell of thick paper.

"So now Mama received seven," said Velvel.

"Nu, so why are you standing there looking at me like two potatoes?" Zev had already climbed back onto his horse. "Take it! Run! Deliver it to your Mama!"

"Thank you," I called out, as I headed towards our cottage.

"Toba! Wait! You forgot..."

"This letter is important Velvel!" I called back. "Everything else can wait! Come on!" My boots stumbled on overgrown grass and scattered stones. Breathing heavily, I bounded over the rocky path, clutching the letter to my chest.

We ran, racing past Berel Ostrawski, who labored beneath a wooden stick thrown over his shoulders. On both sides of this stick, Berel balanced two buckets of rich milk.

Zushe Michalski sat on crumbling steps in front of his small house, a Gemara in both hands, arguing with our neighbor, Boruch Goldenberg, who waved a thumb in the air.

Velvel was right behind me. We dodged past two scrawny chickens, dashed around a fallen oak and a familiar wooden shack came into view. Bursting through the door, I breathed in the warmth of Mama's potato soup. Three-year-old Luba sat on the dirt floor, lining up a row of twigs.

Zeide hunched over his work table. Fresh new pages of a sefer were spread out before him. He twisted a sharp awl, punching little holes between the pages. He picked up a thick needle, loaded it with waxed thread, and began sewing through the holes.

"Toba!" Mama looked at me from over the soup pot. She splashed her ladle into the soup and raised her hands over her head.

"Where is the clean clothing? The dress? The tablecloth? The river didn't wash it all away like last time, did it, Toba?"

Mama sighed. She wiped her hands on her apron and adjusted the cloth on her head.

"Please tell me you didn't lose everything, again."

I didn't answer. I lifted my hands out, holding the letter like a peace offering.

"Look what I brought for you," I said.

Mama gasped.

"Papa," she whispered.

I rushed to place the letter in her outstretched palms. A letter from Papa was more precious than a milking goat.

I hadn't seen my Papa since I was eight years old. I remember one of the last times I saw him. I had been feeding stale challah crumbs to the chickens. The chickens had pecked and gobbled the crumbs. I headed into the house, collecting smooth stones along the way. I was going to build a small hut for my favorite hen, Elka.

I stumbled up the path to my home, my arms overflowing with stones. At the door, I heard Mama and Papa talking in hushed tones. I stopped in my tracks.

"Times are dangerous for the Jews," Papa had said.

I knew what Papa was talking about. He was talking about the pogroms. Every day, we heard about angry mobs that swept through a *shtetl* just like ours. Pogroms meant the shatter of breaking glass, the shouts of angry villagers, barns on fire. Papa had prepared a hidden room in the cellar for our family to hide, just in case.

I stood still at the door, waiting for Mama and Papa to notice me. The pebbles were heavy. My arms were tired. I saw Mama put her hand to her forehead. "But there's not much can we do about it," she had said. Her large brown eyes looked worried.

"And what kind of life is that?" Papa had answered. "It is too risky to stay here."

"But what other choice do we have?" Mama had asked. I wanted to run inside the house and give Mama a big hug. That would make her feel better.

"I will find another place to live," Papa's voice was strong. "My family will not live in fear. Not if I can do anything about it. I will move to America. I will find work there."

America! I had thought. That must be the name of a new men's clothing shop in Warsaw. Papa would find tailoring work there. He could do wonders with a needle and thread.

My arms shuddered. Pebbles spilled all over the ground.

"Toba!" Papa exclaimed.

Mama shrieked.

"Papa," I had asked, "will you bring me a tiny duck from Warsaw? Or a small parakeet like Perushka has? Or maybe a pony? Just a little one. I'll let Velvel ride it sometimes, really I will."

Papa had smiled at me. But he had not laughed.

Later that night, after the pebbles were all cleaned up, Papa sat down with Velvel and me and told us about America. He said that

America was a far away country, all the way across the Atlantic Ocean! In America, Jews were allowed to learn Torah and live without fear of pogroms. The streets were paved with gold. That was a good thing, because Papa would need some gold to buy me a pony.

One week later, Papa's bags were packed. Just like that, he was gone. Three years had gone by since then. I missed Papa tickling me awake every morning. I missed Papa sewing patches on my dresses after I tore them on a branch or a tree trunk. I missed feeling Papa's strong hands on my head, *bentching* me before Kiddush on Friday night.

I worried about Papa, too. How would Papa chop wood for his fire without Berel Ostrawski's help in the winter? Did he have friends like Boruch Goldenberg and Avraham Livshein to learn Gemara with? Without Mama around, who would take care of Papa if he got sick?

When I thought about these things, I started to feel sad. My eyes would begin to feel wet and a ball would form in my throat. So, I tried to take my mind off of Papa. I would go outside and try to spot white-tailed eagles in the sky. Sometimes, I would visit the chickens and name all the newly hatched chicks. My favorite names were Adela, Aron, Basia, and Boruch.

And now, we had a letter from Papa! Whenever we received a letter from Papa, our family worked itself into a frenzy. Velvel would run around the house and bump into things, until Mama had the letter opened and was ready to read. Zeide always dropped his book binding materials, and inched towards Mama for a better look at the letter. Luba did not remember Papa, but she could feel the excitement and would begin to sing made up songs at the top of her lungs.

What news did Papa send this time? Did he make enough money to bring the whole family to America?

"Toba!" Mama said. "Please pass the challah knife."

I rummaged through the wooden cabinet where we kept our silver, and handed Mama the thick, heavy knife.

Velvel stopped bouncing and crept close to Mama. She slit the envelope with the knife. Zeide put down his needle carefully, and wiped some glue off of his palms. He rested his eyes on Mama as she jammed her hand into the envelope. She pulled out a wad of money and silently counted the bills.

We watched Mama's face as she read the slanting letters on the thick white paper. At first, Mama's eyes lit up. But as she read more, her lips turned down slightly.

"What is it Mama?" My body shook as I shifted from one foot to the other. "Tell us!"

Mama sagged onto a nearby chair. "It has finally happened," she said. Her eyes met Zeide's. I tried to figure out what that look meant. Was it a happy look?

"It happened," Luba said, poking her potato doll in the eye.

I looked back at Mama. "Toba, fetch the

washing. Velvel, help your sister carry everything back from the river. We need to start moving," she said, as if in a trance.

"Mama, what's wrong? Is there bad news in Papa's envelope? Did he find a spider in his house?" Spiders are terrifying.

The corners of Mama's eyes creased and her lips went up a little. That made me feel better.

"No, Toba'le," she said. "No spiders. In fact, there's very *good* news. You and Velvel are going on an exciting adventure in only three days."

"If Papa sent us good news, Mama, how come you don't look happy?" I asked. "You look like you've seen a spider."

"Papa sent enough money for two people to sail across the Atlantic Ocean," Mama said, her voice dropping.

"Two people," I repeated slowly, "Velvel and I are sailing across the sea... alone?" I didn't want to go to America at all. I loved my shtetl. I knew all of the people. I knew all of the trees, the birds, and the rivers. I did not want to go *anywhere* without Mama and Luba.

Mama reached out and stroked my face. Her hands were rough and stained from peeling beets and potatoes.

"Aunt Fronya has some money saved up. She will take care of you and your brother. Luba and I will join you later," she said softly.

"Later?" Tears pricked my eyes. "How much later?"

Mama held my hands in both of hers. I suddenly felt like a very little girl, almost as little as Luba.

"When Papa makes more money."

"When is he going to make more money? How much money does he need to make?" I asked.

Mama dropped my hands. She sucked in her lips and looked around the room. "We have work to do," she said, changing the subject. This is what my mother sometimes does when she doesn't want to answer my questions.

"Toba, Velvel, the laundry."

Mama heaved her body out of the chair. She dragged a wooden trunk from the corner of the room, dropped it in the center, and lifted the cover. It crashed down to the floor with a thud.

———•◆•———

Mama had all of mine and Velvel's things packed up in no time. Three thick quilts were stuffed deep in the trunk. Velvel's second pair of pants and my other dress were folded neatly on top of the quilts. Mama's homemade rolls, four large blocks of cheese, and a tub of sardines were carefully wrapped and knotted inside a sturdy canvas bag. Mama threw in lots of onions. She knew how much I loved those.

"Mama," asked Velvel, "Won't those foods make the bag smell?"

I threw him a look. He didn't appreciate onions the way I did.

"Better to eat cheese and onions than to

eat air," said Mama.

There was no arguing with that.

Even though I was happy with the foods Mama sent, I personally, would have added a pot of warm borscht soup, crunchy potato latkes, and at least four steaming apple cakes.

Mama rushed about, her dark skirts sweeping the dirt floor. She wrapped, unwrapped, and re-wrapped the rolls. She fussed over Velvel's old coat.

For three days, my stomach flip-flopped. I was excited about travelling across the ocean. I would get to see America, with its golden streets. What would it be like to walk on so much gold?

Would my boots slip on it? Maybe American cobblers crafted shoes made especially for walking on gold.

I studied Zeide's face. It was soft and leathery and had many lines and wrinkles. I stared and stared at him, until he looked at me funny.

"I'm drawing a picture of you in my

mind, so I can remember you in America," I explained. Zeide smiled and continued sewing and gluing his sefer, covering it with a green board. I noticed that he kept his head very still.

This is one reason I love Zeide so much. He knows how to pose for my pictures.

Luba danced over to me and held out her hands. "Pick me up!"

I put out a finger. "One minute, the painting of Zeide isn't ready yet," I said.

When I felt sure that I would remember every part of Zeide's leathery face, I bent down to let Luba climb on my back. She held onto my neck with her chubby fingers. I bounced her around on my back until Luba was laughing so hard, I thought she might burst.

On the third day, Mama said, "Toba, we've prepared all we can." I don't know why she said 'we,' because I hardly helped her pack at all. But I did give Luba a *lot* of rides. Mama wiped her hands on her apron.

She handed me a bowl of mashed turnips.

"Feed Luba while I finish up, and then put her to sleep. We meet Aunt Fronya by nightfall."

Aunt Fronya was my father's sister who was taking us to America. She was my favorite aunt, by far. Whenever she came to visit, she brought chunky sugar cubes for Luba, Velvel, and me. She spoke properly and held herself daintily, like a princess in a story. Sometimes, I wished that I would be like her when I grew up, but it seemed that the chances were slim.

I filled Luba's little metal spoon with turnip. "Wheee!" I called out as I flew the spoon over her head.

"Birdy spoon! Birdy spoon!" Luba giggled. She scrunched up her little face and covered her mouth.

"Open wide," I said.

Luba opened her mouth and swallowed the turnip. There was a big smile on her face, and lots of turnip all over her chin. When there was no more turnip in the bowl, I told Luba

I would be right back.

I reached my hand in the potato bin and found a nice, round potato. I covered it with a piece of green fabric from Zeide's scraps.

I hid it behind my back. "I have something very special for you," I told Luba.

"Let me see!" she giggled.

I took the potato doll out from behind my back.

"Baby!" Luba's cheeks dimpled. She clapped her hands in delight.

"Remember your big sister when you play with this," I told her. I wanted to give Luba something that would last, so I also gave her a river stone. It was smooth, and it gleamed a shining black.

"Shiny!" Luba said with delight when I handed her the stone. She curled her little fist around it.

I put Luba down in her straw cot, and stroked her golden curls as I sang her favorite song,

*Dus vet zein dein baruff*

*Torah iz der besteh schoirah,*
*This will be your work*
*Torah is the best merchandise...*

As soon as Luba fell asleep, Zeide beckoned me close. He put down his needle and thread and picked up a thick, red siddur.

He lifted the sefer, kissed it, and placed it in my hands. It was as heavy as a hen.

"What is this for?" I asked, examining the siddur from all sides.

"Toba," said Zeide, his hands resting on the siddur's spine, "this siddur is yours. It was yours from the day you were born."

*Me? No one ever taught me how to read. And now I owned an entire siddur?*

"This siddur was in our family for generations. It was bound by your Bubby."

I was named after my Bubby Toba. I heard a lot about her, but I never met her. She was the best bookbinder in all of Kolno.

Zeide traced the siddur with his fingers. "This siddur was so old, it was falling apart," he said. "Bubby finished binding it just two weeks before you were born." Zeide closed his eyes.

"I was saving this for you all these years," he said. "But who knows when we will meet again? Bubby would want you to have it."

"What about you, Zeide?" I asked. "You should keep it. I don't even know how to read."

Zeide laughed, his voice hoarse. "I think that in America, you will learn how to read."

I laughed to myself. *Imagine that! A girl learning how to read.*

"And besides," said Zeide, "the siddur will tie you to Mama and Luba, to me and all of Kolno. It will remind you that no matter how hard things become, Hashem is with you."

If the siddur would remind me of all of that, I wanted to keep it close to me all the time. I hugged Zeide.

"Thank you Zeide," I looked up into the

furrows and lines in his face. "I still think that it will be safer with Aunt Fronya, or even with Velvel. I'll lose it, just like I lose everything."

Zeide smiled down at me. "No. The siddur belongs with you."

Zeide picked up a stack of papers. They were covered in his neat handwriting. Tiny purple letters ran across the pages like artwork. He must have squeezed the ink recently because I could smell its tart berry scent.

"This is a letter for your Papa," he said. "Please give it to him when you arrive in America." Carefully, he placed the letter between the pages and the back cover of the siddur.

"Can't you bring it to Papa when you come to America with Mama?" I asked.

"I am too old for such a journey."

I squeezed my eyes shut.

"But Zeide, I..."

"Toba, let's go!" Velvel yelled. The sound of horse's trotting grew louder. Velvel stood in the doorway, hopping from one foot to the next. Near him, Mama stood still. Her lips were shut tightly. I couldn't read her expression, but I could see her fingers twisting around each other.

There was so much more that I wanted to say to Zeide. How could he trust me to guard something so precious? I was only a little girl. I squeezed the siddur close to me, trying to quiet the roaring *thump thump thump* of my heart. It was time. Our journey was about to begin.

## Chapter Two: Saying Goodbye

Zev Volf jumped out of the wagon and lifted our trunk as if it weighed no more than a bundle of pine needles. Mama settled Velvel on the seat in the back of the wagon. I followed Mama and plopped down, holding Zeide's siddur tightly. Mama sat between me and Velvel.

"Can't you come with us, Mama?" Velvel cried out, wrapping Mama in a tight hug.

Mama sighed. "I wish," she said. "I will be with you just until we reach Aunt Fronya. After that, I return to Luba and Zeide."

Zeide shuffled over to the wagon. I could hear his raspy breathing as he reached his arms up and placed them on my head.

"*Yivorechica Hashem v'yishmirecha* – may Hashem watch over you and bless you *mein tayereh aineklach*, my dear grandchildren."

"Zeide, will I ever see you again?" I asked. I was scared to hear his answer.

"Only Hashem knows," said Zeide, "But whatever happens, it is all for the good. You'll see."

I held onto my Zeide's neck, hugging him until Mama gave me a sharp nudge.

"Goodbye, Zeide," I said. My throat felt heavy. Zeide smiled at me, and I painted his smile into my heart.

The horses neighed and picked up their hooves. *Clip-clop, skree, skree.* We were on our way. The wagon swayed from side to side. Reb Notkeh's goat staggered across the dirt path. The wind blew loose shingles off of the Ostrawskis' roof. I caught a whiff of Rebbetzin Ostrawski's onion soup. As we passed the shul for the last time, I heard the voices of Zushe Michalski and the Goldenberg brothers, singing words of Tehillim. Their

voices sounded so sweet. Would I hear men singing those same words of Tehillim in America?

"Goodbye," I whispered to my little shtetl.

My bones shook as we crossed a rickety bridge. We rode onward until the glow of a single oil lamp beckoned us. It was the only light coming from miles around. The horses drew our wagon towards its glimmer until we arrived at a neat little shack.

The dirt in front of the house was swept into perfectly round half circles.

Aunt Fronya sat on a small white chair, her feet side by side, her hands in her lap. Her blue skirt was starched to perfection. A tiny gold watch and chain were pinned to the front of her collar, and an ivory kerchief was tied around her face. On her feet, my aunt wore leather boots so clean and smooth, I was sure she had just picked them up from Isaac the cobbler that day.

"Fronya!" Mama rushed toward her

sister-in-law.

"Pesya," Aunt Fronya returned Mama's hug.

Mama held Fronya's face in her hands. I always thought that Fronya's chocolate brown eyes looked exactly like Papa's. I wondered if Mama saw it, as well.

"Thank you for taking the children," Mama said, holding her hands together. "I am blessed to have such a devoted sister-in-law."

Aunt Fronya smiled.

"Who knows?" Mama continued. "You just might find your Yossel in this new land, this America."

Aunt Fronya sighed. She looked upwards. "With Hashem's help," she said.

Yossel was Aunt Fronya's *chosson*. He was drafted into the czar's army shortly after their engagement. Soldiers in the czar's army always picked on Jews and made them miserable. Since Yossel was drafted, we hadn't heard one word from him. But maybe Mama was right. Maybe he did escape to

America, after all.

Zev hopped out of the wagon. He heaved Aunt Fronya's trunk on his back and swung it into the wagon, "Oof," he groaned.

Aunt Fronya dusted her skirt and walked over to the wagon. She reached in, pinched my cheeks, and handed Velvel a sugar cube which he popped in his mouth after a loud *Shehakol.* "How could I let these precious children travel across the ocean alone?"

"Bah," said Mama with a flick of her wrist, "Toba is almost twelve years old! Practically an adult. And Velvel is quite the responsible one."

Aunt Fronya adjusted her kerchief.

Zev cleared his throat loudly. "We must leave while it's still dark," he called from within the wagon.

Aunt Fronya stepped into the wagon, straightened her skirt, and sat straight-backed on the seat. Mama gave Velvel and me one last hug.

"I will see you again, soon," she said, her voice shaking.

Velvel's shoulders heaved. Mama patted his head.

"Velvel, don't cry" Mama said, "Aunt Fronya and Toba will take good care of you. You'll see."

Mama let go of Velvel and held me close. "Take care of your little brother, Toba," she whispered into my hair.

"I will," I said, looking over at Velvel. He looked so small, all curled up in a corner of the wagon. He looked like he needed his Mama.

Too soon, the wagon pulled away. Blinking back my tears, I watched Mama's figure disappear into the darkness. The horses whinnied and the wagon lurched up a steep hill. Familiar dirt roads turned into brambling forests. The howling of wolves made me shudder. Velvel sobbed beside me, and I held him and sang softly.

*In dem Beis Hamikdosh, in a vinkeleh cheyder*

*Zitzt der almoneh bas Tzion alayn,*
*In the Beis Hamikdosh, in the corner of a room*
*Sits the mourner, Bas Tzion, alone...*

Singing the song, I felt strong, as if Mama was with me, telling us that we would be fine. As I sang, Velvel's head nodded off to the side. I smoothed his yarmulka and peyos. I looked up. Somewhere in the woods, a wolf howled. Aunt Fronya reached for my hand.

# Chapter Three: All Aboard!

I could smell the salty, fishy ocean before we reached the harbor. Walking up to the dock, I watched crowds of passengers scurrying about, clutching bags and hauling boxes. Blue-green waters thrashed and whipped against a massive vessel.

Velvel stared up at the towering ship. It seemed like he wanted to say something but just couldn't find the right words.

"This ship must fit one, no, two thousand people!" he said, finally.

I nodded my head. His guess was as good as mine.

"And look at those funny symbols painted onto the side of the ship," Velvel pointed.

"Those are English letters, Velvel,"

I said. I had seen symbols like that on some books Zeide bound for his customers.

"What do they say?"

"How would I know?" I shrugged my shoulders.

Aunt Fronya squinted her eyes and mumbled to herself. "*F, R, E, E*," she muttered.

"Aunt Fronya, you can read!" I stared at my aunt in awe. I didn't know any girls or women who could read.

Aunt Fronya winked at me and continued studying the letters.

"Free-dom," she said, finally, "The *S.S. Freedom*."

Velvel stared at the vessel, his mouth opened so wide I could see his tonsils.

"Come on, Velvel," I pulled my brother along. "You can stare at the ship later."

Hundreds of people stood with us, waiting in line for their tickets. A girl about my age held the hand of a two-year-old with one hand while cradling a baby in the other.

"Zelig is heavy, Mama," she called to a woman haggling with an officer at the ticket booth.

I held on to Velvel, making sure he wouldn't run back to the ship without me. Finally, Aunt Fronya reached the front. She showed our tickets to a man in a blue cap. He pointed us toward the ramp of the *S.S. Freedom.*

Velvel jumped and threw his bundle of carefully packed food in the air, catching it with two hands.

"*Woo wee, wooo weeee!*" he sang while twirling his bundle in a circle. "We're going to sail on the *S.S. Freedom* for weeks! *Woo wee!*"

I was getting a good feeling about this journey. I had a happy little brother, my favorite aunt to watch over me, and a beautiful, strong ship. What could go wrong?

Green waters crashed against the ship. Seagulls squawked overhead.

"*Woo wee!* Toba, look out!" Velvel called.

A large man with long, curly brown hair

lumbered past, crashing right into me. I slid and slipped landing in a dirty puddle. My siddur went flying right out of my hands!

The big man stopped in his tracks. I expected him to turn and say he was sorry, which is what I would have done if I'd pushed someone in a nasty puddle. But he said nothing; he didn't even turn around. He was staring at my siddur with its fine binding and gold-edged pages gleaming in the sunlight.

I dashed over and picked up the siddur, kissing it tenderly on its soft leather cover. I could feel the man watching me, and I shivered. Maybe I should have packed the precious siddur away in my bag, along with the blankets and the onions. I turned around quickly, hoping he'd forget my face.

"Velvel," I said, "I think I've seen that man before. Does he look familiar to you?"

Velvel scratched his head. "Maybe," he said, "I think he came to have Zeide bind a book for him. But I hope we don't see him ever again. He's scary."

"Children," Aunt Fronya called out, waving her hand over her shoulder. "Follow me." We hurried up the gangway after Aunt Fronya, following the *click clack* of her immaculate boots.

She headed toward a flight of wooden steps. As soon as Aunt Fronya set a boot on that first step, a steward put his hand out to stop her. "Sorry ma'am, but I'm going to have to see your ticket," he said.

"Certainly sir," said Aunt Fronya, lifting her chin. "I paid for my ticket, just like everyone else on this ship." She pulled three tickets out of her bag and handed them to the steward. He glanced at them and looked back at her.

"Hmph," he said, twisting his mouth in a knot. "These are steerage tickets." He said "steerage" the way I would say, "spiders."

The steward pointed down a narrow metal staircase. "You need to turn around and head down that way," he said.

I peered down. The staircase led into an

endless black hole. If that was "steerage," let me tell you, it looked *very* grim. Aunt Fronya glanced down the staircase and back at the steward. She seemed uncertain. She turned toward Velvel and me.

"Children, this way," she said.

The steward watched from above as we heaved down a long staircase. Velvel clutched his bundle and I clenched my arms around Aunt Fronya's package. Aunt Fronya hauled Mama's carefully packed trunk. As we reached deeper into the ship, the thick, sweaty odor grew stronger and stronger. I held my breath and sucked in my cheeks. This did not help the smell go away.

Down, down we marched, deep into the belly of the ship. When we reached a grimy narrow passage, Aunt Fronya clutched Mama's trunk so tightly, I could see her knuckles turn white. I wanted to hold Velvel's hand but did not dare. I could not risk dropping Aunt Fronya's only possessions.

The steerage compartment reminded me

of the cellar beneath our house in Kolno, where Mama cured fish. After coating the fish with salt, she would to hang it from the ceiling so it would last all winter. I hated the dark, cold cellar, never knowing when I might bump my head into a hanging piece of fish. I never walked into that cellar without Mama nearby.

I tumbled forward into the cave-like room and shivered. The ceiling was low. A jumble of iron pipes framed the room. Almost every inch of space was taken up by berths. The small space between the berths formed narrow aisles.

Aunt Fronya walked down one aisle, keeping her eyes open for a spot that could hold the three of us. I followed my aunt, when another woman pushed her generous frame through the aisle. The two of us could not pass through at the same time. I had no choice but to climb up on the closest berth.

Clinging desperately to the side, I watched the woman carry a heavy bundle in her arms. A young girl and five smaller children straggled along behind her, each struggling with their own bags and packages. Finally, the family passed. I jumped off the berth and squeezed my way over to Aunt Fronya and Velvel.

"How many people do you think are stuffed into this room?" Velvel asked as soon as I reached him.

"Three hundred and seven?" I guessed.

Aunt Fronya looked around at the filthy surroundings and took a deep breath. She fingered her gold watch, smoothed her starched skirt, then turned to us.

"Let's get settled."

She found a berth with three available levels for sleeping, stacked one on the other. Aunt Fronya claimed the bottom berth. I took the middle one, and Velvel climbed up to the top. We all got busy spreading sheets and blankets from home for some privacy. There were shelves for food alongside the berths. Aunt Fronya put our food supplies in a cloth

bag. Velvel and I helped her push Mama's trunk beneath the bottom bed. I tied a cloth around Zeide's siddur and secured it to the side of my berth so that it would stay close to me.

I was tying a really sturdy knot, like Zeide had taught me, when a terrible grinding sound belted out from beneath the ship. I stuck my fingers in my ears. The ship lurched forward, paused, and crashed down over the waters. Behind me, a woman shrieked. Aunt Fronya lost her balance. The more the ship rocked back and forth, the whiter her face became. She held onto the bunk to keep steady.

Velvel leaned over a metal rail. "Are we... sinking?" His eyes were large and round.

"No, Velvel," I said. "We're leaving the harbor. We're on our way!"

"I didn't think a ship could make me so dizzy and sick to my stomach," said Velvel.

"We are right at the bottom of the ship; we can hear every sound," said Aunt Fronya.

"We should all say *Tefillas Haderech*."

Aunt Fronya said the words of *Tefillas Haderech*, and Velvel and I repeated after her. Velvel nestled into his berth. I curled up into mine. The mattress was thin and smelled of mildew. I heard rats scurry beneath the bed.

I tried to relax my body, imagining what life would be like once we reached America. Papa had written that his name was changed from Czapelski to Shapell. Would I remember to call myself Shapell when I reached America? What type of name was Shapell anyway?

I peered down at Aunt Fronya. She would remember, even if I didn't. My aunt had a perfect memory. But when I looked down, I was suprised to see that Aunt Fronya's hands were wrapped around her stomach. A layer of sweat covered her forehead. She squeezed her eyes shut. "Toba," she said so quietly I had to put my ear next to her mouth in order to hear, "I don't feel very well."

———————◆———————

I must have fallen asleep. When I awoke, the ship was still moving violently.

"Velvel, are you up?"

His face peered down at me, his eyes wide with fright.

"It's just the waves in the ocean. Nothing to worry about."

"I'm not scared," he whispered.

The rocking motion got worse. At first, bags slid across the floor. Then objects were actually flying across the room. I ducked my head to avoid being hit in the face by an apple.

"Storm ahead!" called out a sailor from up above. There was the sound of a board falling down, and then the click of a lock. We were bathed in darkness. "I don't want to be locked down here!" a woman yelled. The wind whistled. The ship rattled like a tin cup.

Carefully, I climbed down to the bottom bunk to check on Aunt Fronya. Her eyes were dazed, and she was moaning softly. This was not good.

Aunt Fronya looked so completely

helpless. How could I take care of her, when it was supposed to be the other way around? I sat beside my aunt and smoothed her hair, pushing it off her damp forehead.

> *Ay lee loo lee loo*
> *Shluf durch der gantzeh nacht*
> *Unter dein keppileh ah malach vart*
> *Shluf shoin tzu*
> Sleep through the entire night
> Under your head a malach waits
> Go to sleep...

I hummed Mama's song, wishing desperately that Mama could be here, telling me that everything would be alright.

I thought of my siddur.

I wanted to hold it, to feel like I was in Kolno. I wanted to feel like Zeide was nearby. I wanted to smell the pages and the leather. I wanted to trace the letters of the *alef-beis* and pretend I could read them.

I tapped around the cold edge of the

berth, but only one empty kerchief hung there, swinging and swaying. I climbed down and felt around beneath the bunk. No siddur. Opening the trunk, I felt through all the clothing. This couldn't be happening. Frantically, I stuck my hand *inside* our food bag. No siddur.

Oh, why didn't I give it to Aunt Fronya? She would have put something so precious in a safer place. What would I do now?

## Chapter Four: Lost

That first night on the ship was long and rocky. I lay awake in my berth, trying to recall where I last saw Zeide's siddur. By now, it could have been anywhere.

Hour after sleepless hour went by. Eventually, the storm passed and sailors opened the doors. A weak beam of light entered the room. The smell of thick black coffee, spicy foods, and sweat mingled in my nostrils. But somehow, I felt steadier than last night. Maybe I was getting used to life on the ship. I lifted my head and said *Modeh Ani*.

It was time to get up and find my siddur!

I washed my hands and wrestled my curls into a braid. Aunt Fronya mumbled in her sleep. I heard Velvel saying *Modeh Ani*.

He didn't sound sick anymore, either.

I grabbed a woolen shawl, wrapped it over my head and knotted it beneath my chin. I jumped to the floor and opened the trunk.

"What are you looking for?" Velvel raised his head. His hair stood out in all directions and his yarmulka lay slanted on the side of his head.

I was so upset about losing Zeide's siddur, I couldn't even get myself to answer him.

Velvel's head shot up, hitting the metal berth above him. He looked down at me with such a hard stare, I felt like he could read my thoughts.

Ignoring him, I kept sifting through the trunk.

"No," said Velvel. "You didn't."

Was it really so obvious?

"*The* siddur... *Zeide's* siddur," Velvel said, "it's lost, isn't it?"

Giving up completely, I allowed my hands to rest. I took them out of the trunk, and the lid fell with a crash. I sat on the floor and put my head in my hands. "I tied the siddur to this post. Could you have thought of a safer place? How can right next to my head not be a safe place?"

"It must have gotten lost during the storm," said Velvel.

I could tell he was trying to make me feel better. But it didn't work. Nothing would make me feel better. The only thing I needed was the siddur, Zeide's gift. The siddur would remind me of Mama's songs, Luba's hugs, the soft ground of Kolno, the sounds of the shtetl.

A low groan escaped my lips. Not only did I lose Zeide's siddur, I lost the letter as well. I was supposed to give it to Papa!

Velvel clambered down the ladder, jumping over the last rung. He grabbed a tin cup and poured dark water onto his hands. He swiped some water on his eyes and mouth before scrambling to my side.

"Well, what are we waiting for?" he

asked, "Let's find it!"

"Not so fast, Velvel," I said. "You must eat before you start your day." More than anything, I wanted that siddur, but I didn't want Velvel to become sick because of me. Hearing myself speak, I thought I sounded just like Mama. The thought made me feel better.

"Oy," Aunt Fronya let out a low groan. She was covered in sweat and her skin was absolutely green.

I bent down over my sick aunt and clasped her hand.

My aunt opened her mouth to reply. All that came out was a gurgle. I put a cup of water to her mouth. She shoved it aside. Her eyes flitted for a few seconds, and then she was asleep. I wiped the sweat off her head with a cloth, unable to think of any other way to make her feel better.

"Zeide told me about something called sea sickness," Velvel was now fully dressed and standing by my side. "Maybe Aunt

Fronya has it."

In Kolno, Mama was known for her healing touch. People used to come to our door when they had cuts, scrapes, aches, and pains. Mama always used to come up with something to make them feel better. But I didn't remember her ever helping anyone with sea sickness. I'd never heard of it before. "Aunt Fronya, what can I do for you?" I whispered. I was getting good at pretending to be my Mama. I needed to grow up fast. Aunt Fronya was supposed to take care of my brother, and she was my responsibility now. Would I be able to take care of her?

"What would Mama do?" I thought out loud.

"Mama would say 'Aunt Fronya. You need plenty of hot tea and a lot of rest,'" Velvel said.

"Mama *would* say that," I told Velvel, kicking myself for not thinking of that first. "I'll try to make some tea and give it to her when she wakes up."

Velvel nodded. I was glad that he liked my idea.

"In the meantime," he said, "Do you have any ideas for finding Zeide's siddur?"

I shrugged.

Velvel shook his head. "We need a plan, a solid plan. Think. How far could the siddur have gone?" He waved his thumb in the air. "Could it have flown across the room and bounced off a wall? Maybe you never actually tied it tightly, and it slid across the floor and under a berth? Maybe a child saw it, and is playing with it. We need to search in every direction, starting close to our beds, and go from there."

Sometimes, my little brother was so smart, I forgot he was only nine years old. I thought the plan sounded exhausting. But it was definitely better than my plan, which was basically, no plan.

"Great idea," I said. "You start looking north, and I'll start looking to the south."

Velvel rolled up his sleeves. "If we find

nothing, we meet back here, and spread out again. I'll search north-east, and you search south-west."

"Alright," I said.

"See you soon," Velvel called over his shoulder.

I walked around our bed. I kept my eyes on the ground. No siddur. I picked up a torn blanket, and peaked underneath it. I pushed a stuffed bag with my foot. There was nothing behind it. I looked around me.

A family sat around a steaming jug of coffee. An old man with a short white beard and white woolen hat poured the jug into a cup with a broken handle. The family formed a line before him, each waiting for a sip.

A toddler in a blue sailor dress held tightly to her mother's hand.

"Excuse me," I asked the mother, "have you seen an old book?"

"No," answered the mother, wiping her daughter's chubby face with a rag.

I looked under beds, behind trunks, and

beneath walking sticks. I found rags, itsy bitsy mice, and rather large mice, but not my precious siddur. I reached the wall, covered in coughing and sputtering pipes. I saw a black creature, about the size of my thumb nail. My heart stopped. A spider! I shrieked and ran back to meet Velvel, my legs flying.

I waited some time for Velvel to return, trying to catch my breath. By the time he arrived my breath was more even. I did not want my brother to see me being so scared of such a tiny creature.

"Did you find anything?" I asked Velvel, as if everything was normal. I saw that Velvel's hands were empty.

Velvel's head drooped.

"Sorry, Toba," he said.

"Not even one clue?"

"Nothing." Velvel's head drooped a little more. I knew he was disappointed that his grand plan hadn't brought results.

Velvel was sweating, and we did not begin the second part of the plan, the part about north-east and south-west. But looking at Velvel, it seemed that he might soon turn green and catch the sickness of the sea from poor Aunt Fronya.

"Come with me," I said. "We're going to get you some fresh air."

Velvel smiled gratefully.

Reaching up by our berth, I found the bread and hard cheese in Mama's bag. I led Velvel towards the dark passage.

We zigged, zagged, and hopped passed snoring passengers.

"Ouch, my toe!" a boy shouted. He turned his red, round face toward us with an icy stare.

"Sorry!" I called over my shoulder.

A woman draped in layers of green and blue cloth waved a metal pot at us, muttering something in a language I didn't understand.

"Sorry!" Velvel said.

We raced away from the crowds and the stale smells.

Up the stairs we scrambled, climbing

higher and higher, toward the crisp air of the steerage deck. I rushed forward and then *slam*, I teetered backwards. A skinny hand reached out and lifted me up, stopping me from tumbling down the entire flight of stairs. I looked up, right into a pair of deep green eyes.

"I'm sorry," said the girl with the green eyes. "I should have been looking where I was going."

"Thank you," I called after her. But she

was already on her way. I watched her go, her bright red braid swinging from side to side. I didn't even have a chance to ask her name.

"Toba," Velvel called out, "what's taking you so long? Come on!" I shook my head and ran up the remaining stairs.

The first sight that greeted us on the steerage deck was a young boy about Velvel's age leaning over the railing. He was staring out to sea.

The boy was so skinny, his body could have been made of matchsticks. His pants swam around his legs.

"What are you looking for?" Velvel called to him.

"Seagulls!" he shouted.

Velvel looked at me, a questioning look on his face.

I shrugged my shoulders. I loved the red birds in Kolno, with their feathered crowns and small black beaks. I loved to watch geese, with their spindly orange legs and oversized bellies, but seagulls? They were just big white birds who squawked and gave me a headache.

"Have you seen a siddur?" Velvel asked the boy, "It's a type of Jewish book."

"No," said the boy, still staring out at sea, looking for those seagulls of his.

Velvel spotted two men sitting on the floor, stuffing their pipes with tobacco.

"Excuse me sirs, have you seen a –" Velvel started.

"Hey, Bartek, look at that. A little Jew, starting a conversation with us," laughed one man.

The man named Bartek turned around. A dark bush of hair sprouted out of his head, falling into his beady eyes. It was the man from the wharf! It was the same man who had pushed me over and into a puddle! He was sitting with his friend, playing a game of cards.

"To what do I owe the pleasure?" Bartek turned around.

Was the man really willing to help us?

I felt a surge of hope rising within me.

"We're looking for a book, sir," I said.

Bartek's eyes gleamed. "Oh, a book," he said.

A sudden flash sparked from his eyes. I shivered.

I nudged Velvel in his arm and shook my head. I didn't trust this man. We could find other people to help us.

"Actually," I stammered, "I made a mistake. I don't need anything. I think we found the book already."

"I know you're looking for something, Jew," Bartek put his hand through the curly hair at his scalp and scratched vigorously. "I've been watching you question all the folks on this ship about some book or another. You can trust me. I can help you."

"Really, sir?" Velvel's eyes brightened. "That would be so kind of you."

*No Velvel!* I thought to myself, *don't tell the man anything!* But I couldn't stop Velvel. He was so trusting.

"We're looking for my Zeide's siddur," Velvel's eyes were bright.

"*Velvel!*" I yelled at him in my head, "*Stop! You've said enough!*"

But Velvel went on, "We lost it."

Bartek smiled. His eyes pinched together and shrunk into tiny black grooves. He scratched the hair behind his ears.

"Hmm," he said. "It's a good thing you told me. You see, I am a collector of old books." Bartek puffed out his chest. "I collect and sell precious, ancient books. The older, the better. The older, the more precious. You can make a lot of money selling old books, you know."

Bartek raked his hand deeper into his hair. "So let's you and me make a deal. If you find it, you keep it." Bartek smiled. It was not a nice smile. "But if I find that old book," he sneered, "it's all mine."

Velvel looked shocked.

I turned away. I couldn't believe this was really happening. All I wanted was to find the siddur and survive the rest of the trip to America. How did I allow this Bartek fellow to get involved?

"Come on, Velvel," I pulled my brother aside. "Don't talk to that man."

"Like I always say," Bartek called after us, "finders keepers; losers weepers."

Bartek laughed again. The sound chilled my bones like an icicle in the winter. I hurried away, Velvel beside me. My heart was pounding like a laundry bat on rocks. I needed time to think.

I walked over to a stash of overturned crates. A girl sat on a crate, painting foaming blue and grey waves onto a large piece of wood. The painting looked so real, I felt like I could reach my hand into the painting and feel the water rushing over my fingers. I felt shaky and nervous. Her waves looked calm and soothing.

Velvel turned a nearby crate upside down and sat on it. I pulled a chunk of bread out of my pocket and ripped it into two pieces, handing one to Velvel. He divided his piece of bread into two halves.

I raised an eyebrow. Aunt Fronya was too sick to eat bread. It was hard enough to get her to drink even a tiny drop of water. "What are you doing with that second half?" I asked Velvel.

"Look over there." Velvel pointed to the boy looking for seagulls. The boy's cheeks were sunken in. His skin was a sickly yellow.

"He looks like he needs the bread more than I do," Velvel said.

I gazed after my brother as he walked over to the boy and handed him half of his bread. The boy's face broke out in a wide grin. Watching his happiness, I thought of Mama. Our Mama insisted on having guests for Shabbos even when food was scarce. Mama always sent Velvel and me to shul with some food for a lonely person who needed a meal.

"Thank you, Velvel," I said.

"What for?" We were looking for water to wash our hands.

"For inviting a guest to share our food."

Velvel's face brightened. "Like Mama would do."

I nodded. We both washed, then sat on the overturned crates in silence, watching the roll and rippling of the sea.

We finished eating our bread and I reminded Velvel to *bentch*. We would have remained on deck longer, but it didn't feel right to sit there while Aunt Fronya lay sick and dizzy below. Velvel and I headed back down the ladder to steerage.

Along our way, Velvel kept searching for the siddur.

"Did you see our siddur anywhere?" Velvel asked a small boy who was feeding a baby some mashed up potatoes. The boy looked up. Potatoes dribbled down the little girl's chin and onto her dress. The boy caught the drops, scraping them up with a metal spoon.

"What's a siddur?" the boy asked, wrinkling his eyebrows in confusion.

"It's a holy Jewish book." I answered.

"That's funny," the boy said. He filled the small spoon in his hand with more potato. "A man with long curly hair asked me the same thing just a few minutes ago. Are you two looking for the same book? Is that man your grandfather? You don't look alike."

Velvel looked at me, his eyes wide.

"No, no!" I shuddered. Bartek had gotten a head start. I had to find Zeide's siddur before Bartek found it, or I would never see it again.

## Chapter Five: America at Last

Days went by. People lay in steerage, moaning and ill. Aunt Fronya's skin became slick and pasty. She was still unable to stand up and get out of her bed. Every day, I poured droplets of water into her mouth and tried to get her to eat.

Our search for the siddur continued. My little brother worked out a routine. Every morning, we split up and searched the floor of the ship in different directions. Still, each night, we returned to our bunks empty handed.

On the fourteenth day of our trip, I had given up.

"Come on, Toba," said Velvel, "We need to keep looking. There is still hope. I'll bet we can find it today, if we look hard enough."

"Alright, Velvel," I said, "But we both know the siddur is gone." It hurt me to say those words. Looking at Velvel's face, I could see that they hurt him too.

"Well, let's search one more time," I added. I didn't want my brother to give me that sad look anymore.

I turned around to start my search when I was hit by a roar of voices. All around me, people suddenly flocked towards the deck, shouting. Men, women, and children swarmed up the stairs.

I raced after them. "Come on, Velvel! Let's see what's going on!"

"Toba," Velvel's voice shook, "is there a pogrom on the ship?"

I turned around and softened my voice. "No, Velvel," I said, "In America we won't need to worry about pogroms anymore. We won't need to worry about people throwing stones because you're a Jewish boy. In America, we will be safe. That's why we are going there. Do you understand?"

Velvel's face relaxed. He nodded and gave me his hand.

"Now let's go see what's happening!"

By the time we reached the deck, it seemed like every person on board the *S.S. Freedom* was on that platform, vying for a space.

Velvel said something. But so many people were shouting around me, I could just see his lips moving.

"Louder!" I yelled.

"How many people do you think are here on deck?" Velvel asked me, raising his voice.

"One hundred and fifty-three!" I yelled.

"That's a lot of people!" yelled Velvel.

"Yes, a whole lot!"

A group of boys standing right by the deck rail was cheering and whooping. I thought I recognized one. I looked closer and recognized the boy who was looking for seagulls.

"That's the boy you shared your bread

with," I told Velvel.

"What is he hollering about?" Velvel asked.

"I see birds!" the boy shouted, "seagulls!"

I looked up at the sky. Large white birds with black wing tips flew overhead.

"Seagulls!" he cried again. "We're nearing land!"

"There's the statue!" a boy next to him roared.

"Lady Liberty!" The crowd cheered.

I wanted to stuff up my ears to protect my poor ear drums, but at the same time, I wanted to know what was going on.

A man stood on a crate, pointing a finger upward. "There!"

"I can't see it!" A girl near me whipped her head around. Her yellow hair slapped me in the face.

"Ouch!" I cried. She stood on her tiptoes, nearly crushing my toe.

"We're here! Finally!" The man on the

crate pointed.

I gazed in the direction of all the pointed fingers.

"Toba," yelled Velvel, "What's going on?"

I clasped Velvel's hand so we wouldn't be separated.

"I see it!" I yelled, "I really see it! Look over there! We've arrived! The Statue of Liberty! Ellis Island! America! We're there!"

You mean we're *here*!" shouted Velvel. "America! America!" He jumped up and down, trying to catch a glimpse of the famous statue.

I stood on my tiptoes. I had heard about the Statue of Liberty before. I knew it was a symbol of freedom, a symbol of a new life, a safer life. Standing on an island amidst blue waves stood the tall green lady. She held a book in one hand and a torch in the other. She wore a crown on her head.

Tears filled my eyes. "She's beautiful," I whispered. I stared at the statue and painted

a picture of her in my mind. It was the prettiest painting I had ever thought up. I concentrated extra hard so that I would remember this moment forever.

*Boruch Hashem!* We made it! Our journey was over. Next stop, Papa!

"Look out!" screamed Velvel.

The girl with the yellow hair lost her balance. With a bang, she fell over my foot. I tripped over a piece of wood, crumpling to the ground, head first. My legs shot into a crate of rotting apples, scooting it across the deck. Before I knew it, crowds of people were falling over each other like dominoes.

"Ouch!"

"Oof!"

"Watch yourself, little girl!" yelled a large woman in a checkered dress.

The girl with the yellow hair glared.

Slowly, I stood up and brushed off my skirt. Just then, I saw a page covered with purple writing floating through the air. Bells went off in my head.

"Toba! That paper!" Velvel pointed. "That's a page from Zeide's letter!"

Velvel held on to his yarmulka and started running, trying to catch the paper. "If a page of Zeide's letter is here," Velvel panted, "Zeide's siddur must be close by!"

Velvel squeezed through a group of squabbling children and hurled himself towards the runaway page. I chased after him. The paper was almost in his hands when a large arm appeared, snatching it out of the air.

"No!" I cried out.

I lifted my eyes, and looked straight into the eyes of Bartek. Bartek's hair had grown even longer since I last saw him. It now came all the way down to his collar. How did his hair grow that fast?

"Uh, uh, uh," Bartek wagged his finger and then stopped to scratch the crown of his head.

"This paper, it's mine."

"But that paper belonged to my Zeide!"

Velvel's face turned purple, almost the color of Zeide's ink.

"If you'll excuse me," Bartek said, a smile painted on his face. Bartek turned on his heel and seemed to melt into the crowd, with that page of the letter clenched in his fist.

Velvel's shoulders drooped.

"Sorry Toba," he said. "I couldn't do anything. One page of Zeide's letter is gone."

I patted Velvel on the back. "You did your best. There will be another chance," I said. "You'll see."

"I doubt it," said Velvel, his eyes surveying hoards of passengers. "If we don't find the siddur now, we won't see it again."

I understood Velvel's despair. Until now, I was sure that we would somehow find it before we landed in America. Once we landed, there was no telling where the siddur could be. The thought of never seeing it again was too much to bear.

Velvel stopped talking. All at once, his eyes widened. I was sure he had another complicated idea up his sleeve.

"That girl!" Velvel pointed to a girl about my age. Her flaming red hair was tied in a loose braid that reached all the way down her back. It was the girl we had bumped into on the deck! I remembered her eyes, green as the forest.

"That girl has Zeide's siddur."

"What? How do you know?"

"I'm telling you," Velvel insisted. "I saw it! I saw it in her hand!"

Near the gangway of the ship we spotted the red-headed girl. She carefully tucked something into her plain canvas sack.

"Over here! Hello!" Velvel and I shouted and waved.

"All aboard the ferry to the Main Building on Ellis Island! All aboard!" A deep voice rang out.

We kept yelling and waving, but the girl was already heading down the ramp toward the ferry. She was taken in by the stream of bodies, all moving in one direction, and then I couldn't see her anymore.

"I can't believe she has Zeide's siddur!" Velvel said, his face flushed.

"It's my siddur now," I said grimly, "and we will get it back!"

## Chapter Six: The Red-Headed Girl

Velvel did a little dance. "It's found! It's found! It didn't fall overboard, it wasn't stolen!"

"Fine. But how will we ever find her in the crowd?"

"We're all going to the same place. Maybe we'll see her in line and can ask her for it. If Bartek had it, we would never see the siddur again."

My heart swelled. Velvel was right. Our chances of finding the siddur were better if the girl had it.

I smacked my forehead. "We can't go after the girl now. We need to help Aunt Fronya out of the ship!"

Velvel and I pushed against the wall of people leaving the ship. Heading down to steerage for the last time, we pinched our noses tightly between our fingers. Aunt Fronya lay in her berth, her body so emaciated, she was a different person from when we first boarded the vessel just a short time ago. Her eyes looked huge in her pale face.

"Velvel, Aunt Fronya can lean on me. You take the bags." I grabbed hold of my aunt's limp arm. Hoisting her weight on my shoulders, we plodded up the stairs together, into the light.

When we reached the deck, officers were striding around, barking orders and directions. The deck emptied as officers ushered everyone onto the ferry boat.

Aunt Fronya, Velvel, and I lingered, waiting for all of the passengers to exit the ship. An officer herded us across a creaking wooden plank and onto the ferry. A woman to my right gazed around her, her arms draped across the shoulders of a little girl.

"Imagine, Karina," the woman told the

girl, "in just a few short minutes, we step onto the Land of Hope."

The girl smiled dreamily.

I stood on the ferry, staring open-mouthed at the massive buildings of New York. Sea water sprayed up at my face. The wind blew around my face but it could not move my stiff, matted hair. I stood still, taking in the chatter of the languages around me, the squawking of seagulls.

After gliding across the harbor for a few short minutes, the ferry pulled up to a tremendous building. An officer ushered us across a rickety plank. My feet swayed as if the earth were moving. How odd it felt to stand on steady ground! I had been dreaming of this moment for weeks now. I leaned into Aunt Fronya. I could see some color already returning to her face. Just standing on land seemed to be doing her good.

There was wonder on Aunt Fronya's face. "We made it. We are here. America!" She smiled slightly. "You children took good care of me!" I was glad that my aunt could talk, glad to have her back.

I was sure that things were going to get better now. Nothing could go wrong in America.

A group of men paraded off the barge, singing and kicking their feet high in the air. A man waved his arms excitedly as his bowler hat fell and plunged into the water. An older gentleman used his walking stick to fish the soggy hat out of the river.

A woman in a striped apron counted and recounted her nine children. A young mother wearing a baby in a sling across her stomach adjusted a large bag tied to her back. A dimple-cheeked boy walked by, a huge bundle resting on his shoulder.

We all headed in the same direction, towards the looming building before us. Aunt Fronya, Velvel, and I stepped into a massive maze of a room, with passages of iron railing. Thousands of people from different ships and countries stood between the railings, forming hundreds of lines. The room was crawling with people. Velvel covered his ears.

"How many people?" he mouthed at me.

I laughed. I couldn't even count this many.

"Around thirteen thousand, nine hundred and sixty-six?" I guessed.

Aunt Fronya tugged on my sleeve. I let her lead me into a line between two iron bars.

As the three of us made it further down the line, I could see the thorough medical exams taking place at the end. I craned my neck. An officer examined a girl who looked about fifteen years old. The officer looked over her head, face, neck, and hands. He nodded. He asked the girl to walk around a bit.

"That's to make sure she doesn't have a limp," Aunt Fronya said when she saw my questioning look. Another inspector used a small metal tool to lift up the girl's eyelid, pull

it back, and peer beneath it. The girl grimaced.

"They're looking for eye infections," whispered Aunt Fronya.

The inspector made a mark on his file of papers and nodded.

"Next!" he called out.

I squirmed. I didn't want my eyelids to be lifted like that. Just viewing the inspection made my skin crawl.

I shuddered and turned away. Suddenly, in the sea of black and brown hair, I noticed a blaze of red. It was the girl from the ship! It had to be! I pushed my way through the line, heading towards the girl with Zeide's siddur.

"Toba!" Velvel and Aunt Fronya called out.

"What do you think you're doing?" a woman shouted.

A pair of hands tried to stop me. I pushed through.

"Back in line," ordered a man in uniform. "Stand quietly, or we'll send you back to Poland."

I gulped and stood still. Tears filled my eyes. I made my way back to Aunt Fronya and Velvel. "I saw the girl, but I couldn't speak to her," I told him.

"But let's watch where she goes," answered Velvel. "Maybe we can catch up to her."

From a distance, we watched the red-headed girl step up for her eye exam. The doctor lifted the girl's eyelid and frowned. He shook his head and marked her coat using a piece of chalk.

The girl's hand flew to her mouth and she looked like she would burst out crying. A nurse took the girl's hand, patted her on the shoulder, and led her to a nearby room. The girl disappeared from our sight. Where was she going? Was she going back to Poland? Did she sail here for nothing, after all?

Biting my lip, I turned back to Aunt Fronya and Velvel. Not only had I missed my chance to get the siddur back, but now I felt terrible for that poor girl.

We inched closer and closer to the front of the line.

Soon, it was Velvel's turn to be inspected. My brave little brother didn't wince as his eyes were checked. The inspector smiled. Velvel's eyes were fine! Next, he listened to Velvel's chest and nodded his head. The inspector motioned for Velvel to open his mouth wide. The inspector made a check on his paper. Now it was my turn.

I stood still, feeling the cool metal touch my eye. The doctor checked my mouth, hair, and hands. I walked back and forth to prove I didn't limp. The doctor nodded.

But he did not nod at Aunt Fronya. The doctor frowned at Aunt Fronya's thin face. He shook his head when he looked into her throat. The doctor marked her coat with an American letter.

My heart dropped all the way down to my toes. Would our aunt be forced to go back to Poland? Would the officers allow two children to enter America on their own? Terrified, Velvel and I followed a nurse to another room.

I must have looked miserable, because the nurse in a white outfit and a triangle hat smiled down at me. She placed two smooth orange balls in my hands. I looked at her, a questioning look in my eyes.

Trying to be polite, I threw one ball on the floor. That should show the nurse that I appreciated American toys.

"What type of ball is this?" I asked Velvel. He shrugged his shoulders. I picked the ball up off the floor, "it doesn't even bounce."

The woman laughed. "*Oh – range*," she said slowly. Velvel and I stared open-mouthed as she dug her thumb into the ball, peeling a layer away. The underside of the peel was white and soft. A colorful food was right beneath the skin. I breathed in the tangy smell. The woman broke the round ball into sections with her hands. I had never seen anything like it.

Velvel stopped a Polish speaking nurse, and asked her where this *oh-range* came from. She gave him a funny look and answered, "From a tree."

Velvel nodded. "The *brocha* is *hu-aitz*," he told me. I took a section of my fruit, and recited the *brocha*. I put it in my mouth and bit down. "Mmmmm!" The juice tickled my chin. Velvel peeled his fruit. His eyes were filled with wonder at the burst of flavor. This was the most wonderful food I had ever tasted!

I pointed towards my aunt. "May I have one for her?" I asked.

The nurse handed me another round ball. I held onto it as the doctor re-examined my aunt. I would hold it all day, if I had to. In America, things would be different. I would find Zeide's siddur, and put it in a safe place. I would stop losing things. I would take good care of Velvel, and Aunt Fronya if I had to. I would be more like Mama.

## Chapter Seven: A New Life

Velvel, Aunt Fronya, and I stayed the night at Ellis Island. A nurse escorted us into a room jam-packed with people. Metal beds filled the space from wall to wall. I looked around for the red-headed girl, but she was nowhere to be seen. As I lay in bed worrying about Aunt Fronya's health, people trickled in until there was no space left to stand. People settled down to sleep on the floor because there were not enough beds.

By the time we woke up, Aunt Fronya looked better than she had the day before. Some pink coloring had returned to her cheeks. At Aunt Fronya's second checkup, the doctor announced that she was improving. We were going to meet Papa!

But still, we were not through with Ellis

Island. Velvel and I followed Aunt Fronya into a room filled with gleaming wooden benches. The room was crowded with men, women, and children. The room was still, aside for the sounds of scratching pens.

Four men in suits and ties sat behind a high wood desk. One man tapped a pen on his front teeth. He looked down at us and crooked a finger. Aunt Fronya shuffled to the front of the room. Velvel and I followed.

"Where are you from?" he asked. His teeth were lined up like two perfectly straight stripes. They were so white, light reflected off them.

"Poland," said Aunt Fronya, "don't speak English."

Beside the man with the teeth sat an officer twirling the ends of his mustache. It curled up into two sharp points.

"Who is going to be responsible for you three?" he addressed Aunt Fronya in Polish.

"My brother is responsible for the children and me. He is their father," Aunt

Fronya answered.

"And what is your last name?"

"Czapelski," answered Aunt Fronya.

The first man straightened his tie. He tapped his teeth.

I tugged on Aunt Fronya's skirts. "Shapell," I whispered. "Papa's name was changed to Shapell."

Aunt Fronya cleared her throat.

"I-I mean Shapell," she told the men. "We are Family Shapell."

The man scanned a long list before him. His eyes ran down, down the list and then stopped. "Ah," he said.

Dipping the pen into his inkwell, he scrawled large letters on the form in front of him. Finally, he looked up at us. He waved his pen in the air.

"Welcome to America!"

Velvel, Aunt Fronya, and I walked into a large hall. It echoed with laughter and joyous voices. My body relaxed. It felt like years since I had heard so many sounds of happiness. Children jumped into the arms of older relatives, relief shining in their eyes.

An old man stood still, holding a dented trunk. Tears ran down his face as four little girls came running towards him.

"Grandpa! Grandpa!" The girls laughed, surrounding their grandfather. Their mother and father looked on as he handed each of them a carved, wooden doll.

The girls wore round straw hats with huge bows, and their long hair flowed freely around their shoulders. Golden earrings gleamed in their ears. This must be how American girls dressed. I touched my limp hair and looked down at my outfit. I wore all black. My clothes were wrinkled and not too clean.

Aunt Fronya smoothed her skirts. Velvel straightened his cap. I smoothed down my matted hair and quickly braided it as best I could.

I hadn't seen Papa in three years. What if he looked so American that I wouldn't recognize him? What if Papa didn't recognize us? After all, Velvel and I had grown a lot in the past three years.

Aunt Fronya, Velvel, and I sat, watching families unite, one after the other.

Papa was nowhere to be seen.

"When is Papa coming?" asked Velvel.

"Maybe he's here but we just don't recognize him," I said, hoping that I was wrong.

Velvel looked up at me, hurt. "Papa will always recognize me," he said. "And I'll always recognize him."

"Toba'le! Velvel!" a voice boomed.

From across the room, I spotted a dear face with chocolate brown eyes.

"Papa, my Papa!" cried Velvel.

"Papa! It's really you!" I whispered.

Papa stood out in a crowd of beardless Americans. Up close, I could see that his beard was laced with grey. A large yarmulka covered his head. A long, woolen *bekesheh* covered his white shirt. Papa ran towards us, his *tzitzis* flying. He lifted Velvel in a bear hug, twirling him as if he weighed nothing at all.

Papa lowered Velvel and squatted down, looking straight into my eyes, "And how is my *zeeseh maydeleh*?" he asked.

This was my Papa! The Papa who fixed my torn dresses, the Papa who bentched me on Friday nights. Seeing Papa again was a dream come true. But I suddenly felt shy. I was so much older now. When Papa left, I was a little girl. Now, I had been taking care of Velvel and Aunt Fronya on my own for weeks. I looked down.

"Fine, *Boruch Hashem*," I said quietly.

"I see you've taken care of your little brother," Papa patted Velvel's head.

I smiled and looked up. Papa understood me. He saw that I had grown up. Being with Papa was going to be wonderful.

"Fronya," Papa bowed his head towards his sister, "welcome to America."

Aunt Fronya smiled and wiped a tear

from her cheek.

"Thank you for taking care of my *kinderlach*," said Papa. "I will never forget your kindness."

Aunt Fronya waved away Papa's comments. "They practically took care of themselves," she said, winking at me.

Papa took Velvel by the hand and heaved our bag around his shoulders. I held on to Aunt Fronya as we left the hall. Together, we left Ellis Island behind, ready to begin a new life.

## Chapter Eight: Streets of Gold

The ferry from Ellis Island to Manhattan was just a few minutes long. "Oh no," Aunt Fronya gagged when she saw the ferry, "Another ship?"

When we arrived in Manhattan, the air was thick and gray. Velvel clung to Papa and looked around with wide eyes. America was a marketplace. Men shouted in Russian, Yiddish, and languages I had never heard before. They waved pots, pans, bread and baked sweet potatoes high in the air. I pushed my sturdy boots into the rocky pavement. The boots, so warm and reliable in the cold Polish winters, were boiling my feet underneath the hot sun.

There wasn't a patch of grass in sight. The smells of gases and fumes caught in my throat. Rows of red brick buildings rose high above our heads. I looked up, trying to discover what type of birds flew in American skies. But I didn't see any red birds or geese. I looked down and saw fat pigeons, their eyes round and beady, pecking at the ground.

I was surprised that the street beneath me was not made of pure gold. In fact, it was made up of a patchwork of gray and brown cobblestones.

I struggled to keep pace with Papa.

"I thought the streets in America were paved with gold," I whispered to Velvel.

"We didn't reach the gold part yet," he said confidently, "I'm sure we'll get to it soon."

"Thread! Top quality thread!" A man called out in Yiddish. He smoothed one hand over his thick white beard. Thick eyebrows dipped into his eyes. He looked more like a rav than a salesman. The wicker basket hung around the man's neck, weighing his back down. "Red thread, blue thread, black thread, every color thread. Buy my high, very, very high quality thread."

Ears buzzing, we followed Papa over the scorching pavement, weaving our way in and out of throngs of people. Rows upon rows of wagons lined the sides of each street. Horses dragging wagons full of merchandise clomped down the pavement, giving off a powerful odor. I held my nose tightly.

A pack of skinny chickens squawked, clucking at our shoes. Two girls ran after them, balancing an empty cage between them. "Chickens!" they screamed as the cage rattled, "Catch our chickens!"

A gang of boys stormed past us, their clothing covered in dirt. Ragged suspenders held up ripped pants and torn shirts. Most of the boys ran barefoot, their filthy feet striking the hard cobblestones.

Papa looked straight ahead and turned onto a street with rows of red and white buildings. "Hester Street," Aunt Fronya read the street sign out loud.

"Here we are," announced Papa, coming to a complete stop. "Home, sweet home!"

"But I don't see any homes here, Papa. No barns, no cows, just buildings, buildings, and buildings. Where will we live?"

"Toba'le," Papa said with a twinkle in his eye, "our house is in this building."

I cocked my head to one side and stared at the tall brick building in front of me. Stone trim framed the windows and door. A green metal staircase snaked upwards, creating tiny fenced porches in front of the windows.

"How many windows do you think are in this building?" I asked Velvel, staring at the building looming over us.

He scratched his head. "Two hundred and thirty-eight?" he answered.

"Yes," I said, "Looks exactly like two hundred and thirty-eight."

Did America have grass? Where did food grow? Where were the roosters? How could a person live without the sound of roosters to remind them what time to wake up in the morning? There were no rivers or bushes in sight. Just cobblestones, cobblestones, cobblestones, as far as the eye could see.

Velvel, Aunt Fronya, and I followed Papa into the entrance of the building. I squinted in the dim hallway. Thick dust lined the worn ceiling and floor. A weak beam of light filtered in through a dirt streaked window close to the ceiling. The staircase squeaked as we made our way up three flights. Finally, we stood before a chipped wooden door. "These," said Papa, opening his hands in welcome, "are our rooms."

He kissed the mezuzah on the doorpost. The rest of us trooped in, ducking into the small space. We stood in the center of the room and looked around. A stove, a large machine, and an ironing board left very little room to walk.

A man wearing a faded shirt and red suspenders sat by the window. Carefully, he cut squares of dark material. Beside him sat an older man with a furrowed brow. He pushed a long string of black thread through the eye of a needle. With expert strokes, he secured a button onto a pair of pants.

Sweat poured down the face of another man with curly hair. A tweed cap sloped over his red face as he smoothed a steaming iron over a finished pair of pants. They all looked up as we entered, but quickly went back to their work.

"This is the kitchen, living, and work

room," said Papa, opening his arms with a flourish.

"Who are all these people?" asked Velvel quietly.

"My workers," said Papa. I could tell Velvel was impressed by the way his eyes doubled in size.

Papa pointed to a large machine. "This is my sewing machine. I sew pants and sell them to stores."

In Kolno, Papa used to sew with his two hands and a needle. Shirts, pants, dresses, and skirts. Why would Papa need a machine for sewing? Were his hands hurt? Was it the law in America?

I eyed the hefty machine. Its metal needles and knobs were a mystery to me. "Does everybody in America work at home, Papa?" I asked.

"Most people work in factories," said Papa, "or out on the streets, selling wares."

"Why don't you work in a factory, Papa?" asked Velvel.

"I don't work in a factory because all factory workers must work on Shabbos," Papa said. "Yidden lose their jobs when they refuse to work on Shabbos."

"Aha," said Velvel. "So, you work from home."

"Yes," said Papa. "By working from home, I can be my own boss. I hire as many Yidden as I can so they don't have to work on Shabbos, either. But never mind my work now," Papa said suddenly. "You three must be starved."

Velvel and I nodded. Aunt Fronya smiled, her mouth closed. She leaned against a wall.

"Sit down," Papa gestured towards a bare table pushed against a wall. "Eat something."

Papa took a few steaming potatoes out of a pot of water on the stove. He opened the bottom drawer of a wooden cabinet and took out a large bowl of borscht.

My eyes widened. "Borscht," I whispered.

I didn't realize how much I missed my Mama's delicious, lemony borscht.

"Papa," Velvel said, "Mama never keeps borscht in the furniture! She keeps it in the basement in the summer so it stays cold." Everyone in my family liked their borscht cold, unless it was the dead of winter, of course.

Papa laughed, "Come here, *boychick*," he said, "I am going to show you something unbelievable."

Velvel and I walked over to Papa's cabinet. He opened up the top door. Inside there was a big chunk of ice!

"This is an icebox," said Papa. "The ice in the top keeps everything in the bottom of the cabinet nice and cool."

"Doesn't the ice melt in here?" I asked.

Papa showed us a tray underneath the cabinet. "As the ice melts," he said, "it drips into this metal pan. All we need to do is empty the ice tray when it's full so that it doesn't flood the house!"

Papa was right. This icebox of his was truly unbelievable. "So we don't need to keep meat in the basement to keep cold?" asked Velvel.

"That's right," said Papa. "We can keep foods cold right here in this room."

What other surprises would I find in America?

Eating warm potatoes and cold borscht at an actual table made me feel like I was back home in Kolno. Well, almost. Papa's borscht

was good, but it was missing Mama's touch of dill. When nighttime fell, my stomach was full and my eyes kept closing. Papa led me to a narrow doorway. A thin mattress lay on top of a chest of drawers. I plopped onto it and said *Shema*.

Once I was lying on the mattress, my eyelids refused to stay up any longer. Mama's lullabye floated through my mind.

*Gedenk shoyn kinderlach,*
*Gedenk shoyn tayereh, vus ir lerent du,*
*Zugt shoyn nuch a mol*
*Un takeh noch a mol, kumetz alef uh*
*Remember children, what you learn here*
*Say it again and again, kumetz alef uh.*

It wasn't long before I was fast asleep, dreaming about cobblestones, sewing machines, and Zeide's siddur.

———◆———

I awoke to the smell of frying eggs. Papa sat behind his machine. He greeted me with a bright smile.

"Good morning, *zeeskeit*," he said.

How long was he awake?  When I had gone to sleep last night, Papa was up, sitting behind his giant sewing machine.  You will not believe how fast Papa can sew using that machine.

*Whirr, whirr,* Papa's machine breathed as it stitched two pieces of material together.  It must have taken him twenty seconds to do it. At home, it took Papa a half hour to sew up one pair of pants.  This machine *was* fast!

All at once, I heard shouts and laughter streaming in from the narrow window. Velvel ran to it and stared out. His eyes widened and his mouth hung loose.

"Papa, please can I go outside?" He asked in a pleading voice, "I'll be careful. I won't get lost.  Please?"

The look on Velvel's little face would have been enough to convince me to let him out.  Sure enough, Papa gave in without a fuss.  "Go out and play," said Papa.  "But be sure to be back the minute I call you. And don't get lost!"

"Thank you, Papa," Velvel rushed out the door and down the stairs.

I headed out the door, as well. "Uh, uh," Papa called after me. "Not you!" I turned back and tried to copy Velvel's pitiful expression. Papa ignored it.

"Toba, I need your help inside!"

I sulked. I knew I was supposed to feel proud. Being the older one meant that I needed to help out more. Still, I wanted to go outside. More than anything, I wanted to explore this strange land with no rivers or trees, and only one type of bird. And a lazy bird which hardly ever flew, for that matter. Ach, pigeons.

"She's trying to hide it from me, but I know Aunt Fronya was awfully sick on the ship," said Papa. "She is still weak, and needs lots of hot tea. It will be your job to fetch the water."

But where would I find water here?

There were no rivers or large oceans nearby. I couldn't possibly walk back to the Atlantic Ocean for a bucket of water without getting lost.

"Papa, where is the lake?" I asked.

"No lake," said Papa.

He pointed towards the door. Long strips of dark paint were peeling off the wooden door. I had a strong urge to rip all the paint off.

"You'll see a large courtyard downstairs," Papa answered. "Here," he handed me a bucket.

I lifted the bucket and flashed Papa what I hoped was a winning grin. I was eager to find water from something that wasn't a lake. I was eager to get outside, after all. I walked out the door and down the dimly lit corridor. Down, down the steps I trudged. I shuddered when I realized how similar the stairwell was to the ship's dark passage. I reached the bottom floor.

I walked outdoors, shielding my eyes

from the sun. A tall black pump with a long, thin spout stood in the middle of the courtyard. I was not alone. Beside it stood a little woman wearing a pink shirtwaist and a full skirt that reached down to the floor. The little lady dumped her bucket beneath the water spout.

*Plunk.* She grabbed the long lever behind the spout and starting pumping it vigorously. I looked on, impressed. That little lady sure was a lot stronger than she looked! Water gushed out into her bucket, splattering her brown skirt.

The woman turned around and looked at me. I stood there, holding Papa's bucket against my chest. She smiled and gestured towards the pump.

"Go ahead," she said in Yiddish, "your turn."

I walked over to the pump with my head down. I was used to fetching water from the Lavnes River. After weeks of sitting around on the ship, I didn't think my arms were strong enough to fill the bucket. I reached out and grabbed the pump. I tried to pump the lever down but it wouldn't budge. I tried again.

"You can do it," said the lady, "just push on it with all your might."

I flashed her a grateful smile. It was nice to hear some encouragement.

I pushed all my body weight down and *splash!* Water gushed through the spout, knocking my bucket over. My clothing was soaking wet, but I was as happy and proud as could be. I had mastered the pump! I could bring water up to Aunt Fronya! Many pumps later, the bucket was full. My arms were in pain and felt heavy from pushing down the iron rod. Holding my sodden skirts, I ran up the stairs until I reached the door. Bashing it open with my foot, I called out, "Papa! I did it! The bucket is full! Full to the top!"

Papa sat behind his sewing machine, sewing pins sticking out of his mouth.

"*Nu,*" he gestured, "so where is it?"

I looked down. I had forgotten to schlep the water upstairs. Without a look back, I ran downstairs again. I wiped a bead of sweat off my brow. *Oy!* Why did I have to forget things all the time?

I ran into the courtyard, and found my bucket overturned. I took hold of the lever, pumping water into my bucket again. This time, I knew exactly what to do. My arms shook and wobbled. They felt like shaky leaves.

When the bucket was full, I grabbed hold of the metal handle and lugged it to the fourth floor. I was sopping wet and out of breath by the time I reached the door. Half of the water I pumped had spilled on the way upstairs. I sighed. My bucket was half empty.

I rummaged through a cabinet and found an old handkerchief. I soaked it with water and squeezed it out, then tiptoed over to a sleeping Aunt Fronya. I placed the handkerchief on her head. She shivered when the cold cloth touched her face.

I bustled into the cramped kitchen and plunged a rusty tea kettle into the bucket of cold water. I added coals to the oven, and put my hand inside to check the temperature. When the oven felt hot, I placed the tea kettle on the gas range until it started to whistle.

Aunt Fronya's eyes fluttered. I put out my hand and touched her shoulder. She mumbled to herself. "Aunt Fronya, wake up!" I said. "Your tea."

"Place it here, right on the seam," I heard Papa's voice as he spoke to one of his workers.

My aunt's eyes flew open. She looked around the room as if she were lost.

I mopped her head with a cool cloth. "Shh," I said. "You were having a bad dream. It's just me. Toba."

Aunt Fronya sighed. She reached her hand out for the tea and stared into the hot liquid.

I sat down on the floor close to her mattress and waited until she whispered the brocha and took a sip.

I lifted a strand of Aunt Fronya's hair from her eyes. She barely resembled the perfectly poised young lady she was when we first left Kolno. The trip had been hard on her.

Aunt Fronya patted my hand. Her fingers felt thin and cold.

I tried to distract her by asking a question. It took me a minute until I thought of a good one.

"Do you really think that there is a chance that Yossel is in America?" I asked.

Aunt Fronya stared down at her blanket. "Only Hashem knows," she sighed. But when I get well, I will turn America upside down looking for him, *im yirtzeh Hashem.*"

"What is Yossel like?" I asked, feeling bold.

A smile lit up Aunt Fronya's face. "He is a *talmid chochom*, and he is kind. He treated his mother and father with great respect. And his little sister? He treated her like a princess." Aunt Fronya looked off into the distance. Her forehead creased. "I wonder how she is surviving without him," she said quietly.

"Where..."

"Toba!" Papa's voice rang out over the clickety-clack of his sewing machine.

"Where is your brother? He should have been home for lunch!"

"I'll find Velvel, Papa." I said.

"Take this, before you go," said Papa.

He dug into his pocket and handed me a bright copper coin. I rubbed it between my fingers, feeling its smoothness. My first American money!

I gazed at the coin before tucking it into my own pocket.

I looked back at Aunt Fronya, eager to hear more about Yossel's little sister. But her eyes were closed. I slid out of the room and shut the door gently behind me.

I ran downstairs. A five-year-old girl sat on the stoop of the building, holding a chubby, dimpled baby girl on her lap.

A gang of boys ran about, shouting and

searching behind the barrels and boxes which lined the street. A boy with sandy hair grabbed a round, curly-haired boy out of a barrel and held him by the collar.

"Ring-o-levio, ring-o-levio, one, two, three," the sandy-haired boy shouted on the top of his lungs. He pulled the other boy onto a broken wagon and held his hands up in victory. Four other boys sat on the wagon, wearing glum expressions.

Two boys streaked past me.

"Catch them!" the sandy-haired boy yelled. "Catch the other team!"

A boy scrambled past me.

"Velvel!" I yelled as I caught my brother by the arm, "What are you still doing outside? Papa says to come home!"

"I'm playing with my friends, Toba!" said Velvel, trying to catch his breath. He pulled away from me.

"Ring-o-levio, ring-o-shmevio." I said, putting my hands on my hips. "Get back upstairs before Papa gets upset."

I pulled Velvel back to the building. He pulled away.

A short, stocky boy held the collar of a sandy-haired boy. He began to chant, "Ring-o-levio, ring-o-levio, one, two, three."

"Toba! Look!" he exclaimed. I was a big girl. I did not play chasing games. Well, not anymore, anyway.

"No," I said. "We need to go home."

"Toba, please," my brother pulled on my hand.

Rolling my eyes, I turned around. Why did my brother want me to follow the game so badly?

But Velvel was not pointing to the game.

"It's the girl! Zeide's siddur!" Velvel shouted. Sure enough, the red-headed girl rushed past, holding a wet fish wrapped in old newspaper.

I wanted to go inside with Velvel, I really did. But finally I had the chance to find Zeide's siddur! I couldn't turn it down. I turned on my heels and darted towards the girl.

"Wait for me!" Velvel called out, hanging onto his yarmulka and cap. I rushed towards the fish cart. The smell almost knocked me down.

"Oof!" I covered my nose with my head scarf.

"Toba, don't lose her!" yelled Velvel. "Follow your nose!"

I caught a glimpse of red hair down the road, next to a peddler selling old coats.

"Brand new coats, just one dollar and fifty cents! Oh come on lady, I'll give it to you for one dollar and twenty-five cents!" he yelled, pacing back and forth in front of his cart.

I raced on, Velvel hot on my heels. "Stop, Toba," said Velvel. I stopped and gulped, trying to catch my breath.

"She went that way." Velvel pointed to the right.

"How do you know?" I asked.

"I can trace that fish smell, that's how,"

he answered. That boy sure had a strong nose.

We swung around the corner and skidded beneath a short bridge. Wooden boards clung to each other in the dim light, held by different sized nails. The boards were mismatched, splintered, and moldy.

"The girl went in here," said Velvel. "You think she lives here?"

"Impossible," I said. "A person can't live in a broken down place like that."

"Toba," Velvel laughed. "Have you forgotten the ship already?"

I raised my eyebrows. Velvel was right. People could live almost anywhere. Rotting boards were nailed together to form a makeshift door. I knocked on it. No one answered.

"Knock louder," said Velvel.

I banged until my palms felt sore. Still, no answer.

Velvel nudged the door with his foot.

"Velvel, no!" I said.

He looked up at me and shrugged. The

door swung open.

Inside, blankets were neatly stacked on the floor. A tremendous bucket, about the size of a sheep, sat upside down beside the blankets. A half a loaf of bread and a knife rested on the bucket.

"Quickly! Before she gets away!"

The little girl jumped up from behind the bucket and whizzed past us, out the door. I stood there with my mouth open. That girl was fast!

Velvel and I turned and ran after her.

"Did she go that way?" I asked, pointing towards a little boy selling newspapers, "or that way?"

Velvel shrugged. It was too late. The girl had left her fish in the shack. We couldn't find her without the fish's strong smell. The crowds were thick. Peddlers screamed and customers argued over prices.

"Toba," Velvel said, "didn't you mention something about Papa wanting me home?"

I hit my forehead. "Yes!" I said. How

could I have forgotten to get Velvel home on time? Couldn't I do anything without making a complete mess of things? I stood in a maze of merchant stalls, wondering how to get back to my home.

"Pickles! Pickles! Sour, half-sour, not sour at all, we even got sweet pickles! Pickles!" screamed a vendor.

"Books! Books! Old books, new books, all kinds of books!" That voice seemed familiar. It gave me a bitter taste in my mouth.

A few feet away from me, a cart was piled with books. I inched closer to the wagon. On the other side of the wagon stood a familiar looking man with long bushy hair. Bartek!

"Books! Books!" he called out, a fake grin pasted to his face, "I buy your old books; sell me your new books. A book! A book! Come take a look!"

"Toba!" Velvel took my hand and pulled me away from the book wagon. "Maybe he's selling Zeide's siddur."

I thought I had seen the last of Bartek that day in Ellis Island. It felt wrong, seeing him here, when things were settling down so nicely. One week ago, I was sailing on the *S.S. Freedom,* dreaming about America. I had almost forgotten Bartek and his interest in Zeide's siddur. Did he already have the siddur? Had he sold it?

There was only one way to find out. With great effort, I willed my feet forward.

Holding my head high, I walked over to Bartek's book stand. "Excuse me," I said, putting on a fancy lady voice. "I'm looking for an ancient book." I forced my voice to stay steady.

Bartek looked down at me, lifting one bushy eyebrow. "You! That annoying girl from the ship! I hoped I was rid of you once I landed in America. Off with you! Go steal somebody else's business," he flared his nostrils.

"This cart," Bartek lifted a bright red cloth out of his wagon. He flung it high in the air and spread it over his books, as if protecting them from a storm, "is closed for the day. So, off with you!" Bartek yelled.

Velvel and I turned and ran back home as fast as we could carry ourselves.

# Chapter Nine:  Just Like Mama

I followed Velvel back to Hester Street. How did he have such a good sense of direction?  "Apples!  Red shiny apples!" yelled a peddler.  I pulled a penny out of my pocket.

"Here Velvel," I said, handing my brother the apple. "You must be starving."

"Thanks Toba!" said Velvel.  He made a loud brocha a bit into the apple.

The sound of "Ringolevio one, two, three," told me we were home.

"Hey, Velvel!" a boy stopped chanting and faced my brother, "Where did you go? Our team is winning... Hey! Where'd you get that apple?"

A group of boys gathered, staring at the ripe, red fruit as if they had never tasted one before.

"I can't play now," said Velvel, "my father wants me home."

I led Velvel into the building.

"Those boys seemed so hungry." I told Velvel as we trudge up the stairs. "They looked like they had never seen an apple in their whole lives."

"Boruch is an orphan. So is Chaim. Moish and Ber's fathers lost their jobs." said Velvel as we walked through the door to our flat. "You know what? I don't know if those boys have eaten much of anything today."

I shuddered at the thought. They must be hungry all the time.

"Papa, may I feed Velvel's friends?" I asked.

Papa nodded his head, never taking his eyes off of his sewing needle. "Just like your Mama," he said with a smile.

"Velvel, go call your friends," I ordered. "Tell them all to come in for a hot meal."

I knew how to fetch water; I knew how to boil potatoes. I could make these boys a feast!

Velvel zoomed out to find his friends. I ran downstairs for water. When I got back upstairs with the heavy bucket, I boiled the water on a big pot on the stove. I cut up some beets, carrots, and pickles, which I found deep in the icebox.

I was really impressing myself. I was making a hearty meal for guests. Mama would be pleased with me. I imagined her stroking my hair, telling me how much I'd grown.

A loud knock at the door shoved me from my dreams.

"I'll get it Papa!" I called.

"Shh," said Papa, putting his fingers to his lips. "Aunt Fronya's resting."

"Yes, Papa," I whispered.

I opened the front door slowly, to make as little noise as possible.

At the door, stood a *frum* Yid. He wore

a large black yarmulka. His curly peyos were thick and red, framing a smooth face with high cheekbones. His eyes were deep green. Green as the forest. I was sure I had seen eyes like that before.

"How can I help you?" I asked.

"Is your father home?"

I stepped aside to let the man in. He was a young man, yet he leaned on a cane.

"Reb Yid," said the man looking over my shoulder at Papa, "I hear that you run a *shomer* Shabbos business here."

"Yes, yes, that is true," said Papa, smiling. "Please come in, make yourself comfortable." Papa poured some water into a glass. "Sit while I make you a nice hot tea."

The man granted Papa a tired smile and placed his hat on the table.

"What can I do for you?" asked Papa.

The man sighed. "I was a *melamed* in Poland," he said between sips. "I taught aleph-bais to children. When I first moved here, I landed a few odd jobs. But now, my little sister has joined me in America. And I must be able to afford food and clothing for her. Please help me, Reb Yid."

"Of course," my father shoved his hands in his pocket. "I have something for you right here," Papa reached into his pocket.

"No, you don't understand," said the man, leaning forward. "It is not tzedaka I want."

"No?" asked Papa.

"I come to you for a job," said the man.

"Do you have sewing experience?" asked Papa.

The man looked down and smoothed his beard. "I have none," he said, "But I am a quick learner," he added hastily.

Papa thought for a moment. "I have many experienced workers," he said. "But maybe you can come back later. I will see what I can do."

"Thank you Reb Yid, I will see you tomorrow *im yirtzeh Hashem*," said the man.

"Excellent. And what should I call you?"

asked Papa.

"My name is Yosef," said the man.

Yosef stood up and walked down the stairs.

Shrieks and screams filled the halls. Velvel bounded up the stairs six or seven scraggly looking friends behind him. The boys had holes in their clothing, and many of them wore no shoes. Two boys did wear shoes, but their toes were sticking out in front.

"What did your sister cook for us?" asked one boy.

"Yum, I smell potatoes," sniffed his friend, lifting his nose in the air.

Another boy closed his eyes, and smiled. "I would eat a raw potato if I had one," he said.

I made a face. Blech. Raw potatoes.

The boys washed their hands and sat down at our little table. I sprinkled the potatoes with salt and put a large helping on every boy's plate. Velvel said the brocha with his friends. Silence filled the room as the boys concentrated on the food.

They ate with great appetite, smacking their lips with every bite. I couldn't help laughing. It felt good to see my food making people so happy. Before they left, they thanked me for the simple meal as if I had served something special, like Mama's latkes and apple cake.

I stacked the dishes into a neat pile and handed Velvel a green dish towel.

"I'll wash, you dry," I said.

A green dish towel. Where had I seen this color recently?

It hit me then. I closed my eyes. The red hair! The green eyes! 'My little sister,' the man had said.

"Velvel," I said, "you won't believe this. But you know the girl, the girl with my siddur? I think I found her brother!"

## Chapter Ten: The Search

Velvel stared. "You found the red-headed girl's brother?"

I could tell he didn't believe me.

"Velvel, it's true!" I placed the dishes on the table. "A man came to our door a few moments ago. He wanted a job. He had eyes as green as the forest. Just like the red-headed girl. And his hair was red too, just like hers. He said his name is Yosef."

"A lot of people have red hair, you know," said Velvel, scratching his yarmulka.

"Well, what about those eyes? They both have the greenest eyes I have ever seen. And, he said that he needed to help his younger sister. I'm telling you, that man is her relative."

"And if you're right," said Velvel, "how

can we find him?"

"He did mention that he was going to come back to speak to Papa," I said.

"Aha," Velvel swung his thumb through the air. "Then we must stand guard at the front door. We will take shifts. Half hour shifts. You take the first shift in the morning."

"What time does that shift start?" I asked.

"Five-thirty at the rooster's crow," my brother answered.

"Velvel!" I bopped my brother on the head. "There are no barns here, so you can stop dreaming about roosters crowing. That plan is out. Think up something else."

Velvel smiled sheepishly. There was a knock at the door.

"You get it," Velvel said.

"I'm older; you get it," I said.

"I'm drying dishes."

I puffed out my cheeks, stomped across the room, and opened the door.

My entire body froze. Right before me

stood the man with the green, green eyes. It was Yosef! A kind expression was on his face. No wonder Papa wanted to help this man.

"Hello," he said.

I couldn't answer. My voice was stuck somewhere in my throat.

"I forgot my hat," he said.

I quickly fetched the hat. I turned, raising my eyebrows to Velvel.

"There he is!" I whispered. "See?"

Velvel nodded.

The man turned to leave. My limbs shook.

"Velvel," I whispered, "Now's our chance."

We headed out the door.

"Children, where are you going?" called Papa.

"Out to explore," said Velvel.

"Yes," I said. "This city is so large."

"With so many people," said Velvel.

"And historic landmarks," I added.

Papa laughed. "Shoo! Out with you

two," he said. "Just be home before dark."

"Yes, Papa," we answered.

Velvel and I raced down the stairs.

"There he goes!" Velvel pointed.

We followed Yosef closely. He walked past the man selling fish, and passed the man selling used coats.

"Velvel, he's walking towards the bridge!"

Velvel nodded his head, his eyes sharp, following the man ahead of us.

Yosef walked over to the shack under the bridge, his cane tapping on the cobbletones. Velvel and I stayed far enough away that we wouldn't be seen spying.

"Neshka!" Yosef called out. "Neshka, it's just me. Open up." The rickety door opened up and a little face peeked out from behind it. It was the girl with the red hair!

"See?" I nudged Velvel. I had been right. These two had more than the same color hair. They looked so much alike. They were related, after all.

They talked for a while at the door. I heard him say, "I am going to teach Itche Ber now."

"I'll walk with you," said Neshka. "I have an extra coin. I wanted to buy an onion. Maybe we can have soup tonight."

Now I knew the girl had good taste in food. Onions were the best.

Neshka ducked into her shack and came out with a scarf wrapped around her head. She locked the door behind her.

I put my finger to my lips and motioned for my brother to walk quietly. We followed Neshka and Yosef until they reached a run-down shul.

*Kumetz alef, uh*
*Kumetz beis, buh*
*Kumetz veis, vuh*
*Kumetz gimmel, guh...*

I heard children's voices singing the holy letters and vowels.

Yosef leaned on his cane as he walked into the shul. Neshka turned around and headed towards the marketplace. "A penny! Just one penny for an old lady!" a woman croaked.

I motioned for Velvel to walk faster.

"Neshka!" I called out.

Neshka looked around and then spotted me. She narrowed her eyes.

"Who are you," she asked as she continued walking, "and how do you know my name?"

"A good guess?" I looked at Velvel. "Neshka is a very common name in America." I added.

Neshka's mouth twisted. She was either holding back a laugh, or very annoyed with me. I couldn't tell which.

"Do you have my Zeide's siddur?" I blurted out.

Neshka stopped in her tracks, "What are you talking about?" her expression looked suspicious.

"Do you have any siddur at all?" asked Velvel.

"I do," she said, crossing her arms in front of her. "A lot of people have siddurim. You wouldn't be interested in my siddur. It's not new. It's old, actually."

Velvel's eyes opened wide. "What does it look like?" he asked

"Thick and heavy," she answered, "with gold on the sides of the pages. Why do you want to know?"

That sounded just like mine!

"Does it have some papers in the back, with writing in purple ink? If it does, that siddur is the one my Zeide gave me. It's the one I lost."

Neshka stopped walking and took a deep breath. She looked less suspicious.

"Where did you lose it?" she asked.

"On a ship," I began, "the *S.S. Freedom*, during..."

"...a storm," she said. "That's where I found it! My older brother is a big *talmid chochom*, and he loves sefarim. When I saw this one, I didn't want it to get ruined or left on the ship. Why is everyone so interested in this siddur anyway?"

"What do you mean by everyone?" I asked.

"A man is after it, too," Neshka turned onto Pitt Street. A boy was hitting a ball with a long stick. Velvel stopped to watch, but I pulled him on.

"Did this man have long, curly hair?" I asked Neshka.

"How do you know everything?" she asked me.

Velvel stroked his chin. "Bartek," he breathed.

"I never heard that name," said Neshka. She was walking quickly again. "But a man has been following me around. I think he's after the siddur. That's why I never answer my door. Except for my brother, of course."

Everything was starting to make sense. Now I understood why Neshka had hidden in her home that night when we knocked on her door. She thought it was Bartek, coming after the siddur.

"Onions! Onions! A half penny for two!" Two boys hollered from behind a crate of old onions. I could eat onions all day long, but these onions were brown around the edges. I would not have bought one, even for a penny.

Neshka bought four onions from the boys. It was all I could do not to hold my nose.

"Can we see the siddur?" asked Velvel.

"Of course," said Neshka. "It's yours. Let's go." She waved her hand at us to join her.

We bent over, following Neshka under the bridge.

"I know exactly where I hid it," Neshka said when we arrived at her shack. "I won't be a minute."

Velvel and I waited at the door. It swung open easily. From the doorway of the hut, I could see a large bucket tipped on its side.

Blankets were jumbled all over the floor.

"Someone's been here," Neshka looked stricken. "And the siddur! It's gone!"

I glanced at Velvel.

"Bartek," he said, narrowing his eyes.

I pinched my lips together. "Tomorrow," I said, "we find him and get the siddur back."

## Chapter Eleven: Found!

It was dark by the time Velvel and I arrived home. Papa frowned and told Velvel that if he ever got home this late, he wouldn't be able to play outside again.

"And you, Toba," Papa's eyes showed disappointment. "I expected you to bring Velvel in on time. I thought you were more responsible than this." I hung my head.

"Papa, I'll be more responsible next time. You'll see."

That night, after I said *Shema*, I could not sleep. I kept imagining what it would be like to track down Bartek and somehow get my siddur out of his grasp. Was I brave enough to go through with the plan? It seemed like trouble followed me everywhere I went.

Thoughts of finding my siddur and confronting Bartek zipped around my brain. The apartment was hot and stuffy, and I felt like I couldn't breathe. I pulled my sticky hair away from my neck. Finally, I picked up my pillow, crossed through the workroom, and climbed out onto the fire escape.

I fluffed the pillow and lay down on the cool metal of the fire escape. From where I lay, I could see hundreds of laundry lines reaching between rows of buildings. The clothing seemed to be floating in the air like birds.

Stars winked down at me. I gazed up at the stars and dreamed about my Mama, my Zeide, and little Luba. I imagined that I was resting on the soft earth of Kolno. I imagined the voices of my neighbors calling up to me, singing:

*Aheim, aheim, briderlach aheim*
*Dein mukoim dein menucha*
*Dein eigeneh melucha*
*Home, home, brothers, come home*

*Your place, your comfort*
*Your own kingdom*


I woke up to a blazing sun. Through the window, I could see Papa hard at work, a large pile of finished pants folded neatly beside his sewing machine. He wiped his forehead and scrutinized a pile of black material. Papa never seemed to rest, I realized, even for one moment.

I climbed in through the window and washed negel vasser. I took my dress from the nail where it hung and pulled it over my head. Mama had sewn it months ago, out of some extra blue material. I tried to smooth out the wrinkles. My dark, woolen stockings were developing a large hole in the knee. I would have to darn them in the evening.

"Good morning, Aunt Fronya," I said.

My aunt stood near the stove, pouring water from the tea kettle. She was looking better every day. At last, there was color to her complexion. Her face was filling out again.

"Good morning," she answered. "I just heard a knock. Will you get the door? Your Papa's expecting someone about a job."

I opened the door to Neshka's brother, Yosef, leaning on his cane.

"Please come in. Papa is waiting for you."

But Yosef stood still, as if rooted to the floor. He was looking over my shoulder with a shocked expression on his face. His deep green eyes stared straight ahead.

I turned to see what was behind me. It was only my aunt. She leaned against the wall, as if to stop herself from falling.

Her face and lips were white. I ran to her side. She swayed and sat down abruptly on the nearest chair.

"Aunt Fronya, what is it?"

She didn't answer. Instead, she looked up at our visitor and whispered, "Yossel? Is that you?"

The whirring of the sewing machine stopped. It was if everything stopped. I could hear the beating of my own heart. The room was completely silent.

All eyes were on Yosef as he took a few steps forward. "Fronya! My *kallah*! I thought I would never see you again!"

"Your what?" asked Papa, spitting a pin out of his mouth.

Tears glistened in Aunt Fronya's eyes. "You're alive!"

She began to laugh and cry. I hugged her. She hugged me. Papa hugged Yosef. Aunt Fronya had found her *chosson*!

I busied myself at the stove, pouring large glasses of tea, adding an extra sugar cube into Aunt Fronya's. The adults sat around the table, laughing and talking.

My aunt wiped her eyes. "I didn't know what happened to you Yossel. Why didn't you write?"

"I did write," he said, "but the Russian Army didn't deliver my letters. Once I got here, my letter to you was returned." Yossel pulled a wrinkled envelope from his coat pocket and handed it to my aunt. "You must have already left Kolno on your way to America!"

Her hand shook as she grasped the letter.

Papa smiled at Aunt Fronya. Then he turned towards me. "Nu," he said, "So give your aunt a mazel tov! Imagine! The *Aibishter* brought them together again."

Yossel straightened his back. "But without a job, how can I support a wife?"

Papa thought for a moment. "Pants, you can't sew, but Torah, you can teach. You will be Velvel's *melamed*. You will teach him alef-beis, and Talmud. Just like back in Kolno."

Yossel's face lit up. Aunt Fronya smiled from ear to ear. I hadn't seen her smile like that in years.

Just watching my aunt's happiness made my heart sing with joy. I wanted to tell Mama every detail about what just happened. So I sat down and gazed at Aunt Fronya, painting every detail in my head.

As the days went by, I couldn't stop thinking about the wedding. I had never been to one before. Maybe, once she was married, Aunt Fronya would have a green-eyed, red-headed baby girl. Neshka and I would both be aunts! We would take the baby on walks, feed her a bottle, and sew her little dresses.

I thought about it as I washed the dishes. I thought about it as I swept the floor.

Papa looked over at me, "Just like your Mama," he said, "when you set out to do something, you do it right."

I could feel my face beam. It was true. Mama would be proud. I was taking good care of the family. I put the broom aside and heaved an enormous pot of water onto the stove. Now it was time to do the laundry. I would do it just right.

I turned up the heat until the water bubbled. I put in a handful of soap flakes. After the flakes melted into the water, I threw in shirts and all the white clothing.

I mixed and beat the clothes with a stick. After everything was good and boiled and smelled of freshness, I raised the clothing with the stick, one at a time, and rinsed it in a bucket of cold water.

I lugged the bucket of wet clothes over to the window and climbed out onto the fire escape. Everything had to be squeezed and squeezed again to get all the water out. Finally, my favorite part of laundry day had arrived. I clipped the laundry onto the line and stood back to admire my work. I reached for the last of Velvel's shirts, sweat running down my forehead. It was then that I saw the police.

Oy vey. What now?

Little boys had dropped their bats and were gathering around five policemen in tall white hats. Gold buttons on the policemen's jackets twinkled in the sunlight. The police had gathered around one especially small boy. I leaned over the railing to get a closer look. The police, large sticks in hand, were talking to Velvel!

I climbed through the window and ran downstairs. A small girl sat on the steps with her baby sister on her lap. By now I had learned that her name was Danya. Although she was just seven years old, she knew everything there was to know about our street.

"Danya," I asked, "why are the police here?"

She looked at me. "They are looking for a thief," she said, patting her sister's back.

"What type of thief?" I asked.

"One that steals books," she laughed. "Why would he need all those books anyway?"

"Do you know his name?" I asked.

"Yes, of course," answered Danya. "I know everything. It's Bartek."

I ran towards my brother and the crowd of police. "Velvel, Velvel!" I cried. A large officer turned towards me, tapping a stick in his palm.

"Little girl!" his voice was gravelly. "Do you know anything about the thief?"

I nodded. Now was my chance to find Bartek once and for all!

"Then by all means, show us the way," said the officer.

"Yes, Mr. Policeman," I answered in English.

He smiled. "I'm Officer Glenn."

The other four officers joined Officer Glenn. They looked down at me, expectantly.

"Follow me!" I shouted. I led the officers through the market. Velvel's friends scampered behind and around them. I marched forward. A sweet fragrance drifted from the onion seller's cart. The suit man hollered about new suits and slightly used suits. We passed the fish stand, and a new man selling fresh apple cakes. My stomach growled.

Finally, we reached the spot where the book stand had been. Velvel stopped short. Something was wrong.

"Dreadful!" Officer Glenn bent down to take a closer look.

Dreadful, indeed. Bartek's wagon stood empty. The only sign that anyone had ever sold a book in this place were the few pages that floated in the breeze and lay on the road.

"We may never find this man," said Officer Glenn, examining the pages.

Velvel stepped forward. He knew a lot more English than I did.

"Officer, maybe the man, Bartek, left something?"

"Yes," said the officer, "perhaps he left a clue."

Velvel knelt close to the ground. His friends gathered around the empty wagon. They squatted down, searching for signs on the bumpy cobblestones.

"Look!" Velvel said, his voice brimming with excitement. "I found the cover of a book over here!"

"Here!" said a boy, studying torn papers. "Page two, page three, and page seven. These pages look like they belong together."

"Look at all these addresses written in purple ink!"

*Purple ink! Zeide's siddur had to be nearby.*

The police followed the boys, pursuing trails of pages from many books. Finally, we reached Pike Street. A group of women in ankle length skirts and elegant, flowered hats stood in a group, holding babies and pushing prams. Little girls sat on the stoop playing jacks.

"Excuse me, do you know a man named Bartek?" asked Officer Glenn.

"He has a very loud voice, and he walks like this." Velvel said, lumbering side to side.

"Of course I know him," one little girl laughed. She pointed down the block towards a two-story house with lovely lace curtains. "Over there. The first floor of the DeLuca's place."

A group of children straggled behind Officer Glenn, Velvel and I in the lead. The girls dropped their jacks and joined us. Officer

Glenn knocked on the oak door.

"Open up, it's the Police!" he shouted.

He was met with silence. Officer Glenn lifted his black boot and kicked. The door opened with a *bang*.

We gathered in the doorway, peeking inside. The apartment was a shambles. Clothing and broken boxes were scattered all over the floor. Officer Glenn surveyed the mess.

"It looks like somebody was preparing to escape."

"Bartek," Velvel breathed.

Officer Glenn pursed his lips. "I imagine so, son."

After searching through the apartment, we couldn't find a living soul.

In the corner of the room, I spotted a red curtain hung from the ceiling to the floor. I had seen that curtain before. I rewound the past few days' events in my brain. The red cloth was the same one that Bartek had used to cover his wagon at the market! I walked right over to it.

"Toba! Watch out!" called Velvel.

A spider crawled up the curtain. Usually, I would have jumped and run out of the room. But not now. I was fearless. I put my hand out and moved the curtain aside.

Bartek sat on the floor in the corner, clutching something to his chest.

"You!" He glared at me. "You've ruined everything!"

"Toba, look," Velvel pointed. "There it is!"

Bartek held my precious siddur in his hands, the siddur that took me back to Mama, and Luba, and Zeide. The leather looked soft and buttery. The golden gilt pages shimmered and winked. It looked out of place in Bartek's stained hands.

"My siddur!" I cried. "This man has it!"

Officer Glenn reached out for the sefer.

"No! Don't take this! Do you know how much this is worth? It's worth a fortune! A fortune!" shouted Bartek. "You can take any

other book. I have so many! Let me just have this one, I beg of you!"

Officer Glenn handcuffed Bartek's wrists.

"Sir, all your books will be taken to the station until your trial, except for that one. It belongs to these two brave children."

"No!" Bartek kicked and raged. "Everything's been ruined!" He stomped his feet as Officer Glenn and the other policemen marched him to the paddy wagon.

"All my plans, for nothing!" The officers shoved Bartek into the police vehicle, pulled by two brown horses.

Velvel and I walked home, a crowd of children trailing behind us. I held the siddur, not entirely believing that it was actually in my own two hands! I hugged it close and breathed in the smell of its pages. I was given a second chance, and I would never lose it again.

## Chapter Twelve: The Greatest Gift

For the next few days, everyone spoke about the brother and sister who saved a valuable siddur. Velvel and I were the most famous kids on Hester Street.

"Is it true that you found a thief all on your own and schlepped the siddur right out of his hands?" a boy asked Velvel.

"Did you really find the siddur underneath a bridge after tracking it down with seventeen policemen?" a girl asked me. Some of the stories had gotten out of hand.

Neshka and I told the true facts to everyone who was willing to listen. The two of us had became good friends. In fact, we were so close that I taught her how to make Mama's famous potato latkes. We planned on serving them at Aunt Fronya and Yossel's wedding.   I, Toba Shapell of America, had a best friend. And I was going to teach her to be a great cook, just like me.

One day, after frying a lot of latkes, I took the siddur from its special spot on the shelf. We climbed out the window and onto the fire escape. Neshka took the siddur in her hands and caressed the pages with the tips of her fingers.   She opened the thin pages, pretending that she could read them.

"I wish we could read the siddur by ourselves," said Neshka.

I nodded.   "After all we have gone through to save it."

Neshka gave the siddur a kiss and then handed it back to me.

I pushed it back at her.

"You keep the siddur," I said. "Take it home with you."

Neshka's eyebrows shot up.   "No Toba, this siddur is yours. You searched for it for so long!"

"And you protected it from storms and

thieves," I said, "You keep it. It's what Zeide would want."

Neshka shook her head. "No," she said firmly, "your Zeide wanted you to keep it. He gave it to you, not to me."

"But I want to give you something," I said. Didn't people give things to their friends? I had nothing to give besides for a few recipes for apples, beets, and potatoes.

"You did give me something," Neshka smiled broadly. "You gave me a best friend."

The sun had set, and stars twinkled overhead. I looked up, and was sure I could see Zeide's eyes sparkling down at me.

———◆———

Time passed. My neighbors were talking less and less about the exciting siddur rescue, and more and more about starting school, mending hand-me-down jackets, and building sukkas. Yossel went right to work, teaching alef-beis to Velvel and his friends around our little table near the stove.

As I cooked soup, beets, and potatoes for

the boys, I realized that I had a great opportunity. So, I listened in to their alef-beis lessons. It slowed my cooking a bit, but I was picking up the alef-beis letters and all their sounds. I was sure Zeide would have approved.

I shared all this knowledge with my new best friend, of course, because that's what best friends do. Neshka and I davened from the siddur every day, thrilled whenever we were able to make out a new word on our own.

Our words must have reached straight to Hashem, for sure, because one day, Papa told Velvel and me that he had a surprise. Papa had finally made enough money to pay for Mama's passage to America!

———◆———

The night before Mama's arrival, I cleaned the house until it sparkled. I bought a bit of plaster and stuffed up the small cracks in the walls. I mended my woolen tights and the ripped knee in Velvel's trousers. I bleached and starched Papa's and Velvel's white shirts until they were as white as a pair of doves and as stiff as sheets of metal.

In the morning, I smiled at my reflection in the mirror. My mended tights were black and perfect beneath my double petticoat. I put on my new straw hat. It made me look so fancy. Would Mama think so, too?

When Velvel and I were dressed, we made our way out to Hester Street. Danya sat on the front stoop, singing to her baby sister who was snuggled in her lap.

"Hello, Toba!" she called as I passed. I waved cheerfully.

"Good day, sir," Papa tipped his hat to Officer Glenn, who was strolling down the street. The officer touched his police cap. He smiled and winked at Velvel and me.

"*Ah gutten tug!*" Papa greeted Yaakov, the fishmonger. I held my nose as we passed his fish stand. Yaakov smiled our way, holding two slippery fish in the air. We smiled back, but I kept my hand on my nose.

"A penny a pound!" he called out.

"Special for you, because I like your family!"

We walked the cobblestone streets until I no longer recognized the vendors behind the horse-drawn carts. We finally arrived at the ferry to Ellis Island.

Feeling the boat rock beneath me, I remembered my passage across the ocean. I remembered arriving in America hungry, tired, and confused. But now, I knew my neighborhood and all its secret streets and side roads, and I would show Mama.

I looked around me at the hordes of people streaming out of Ellis Island.

"How many people do you think are here?" I asked Velvel.

"Seven thousand and thirty-eight?" he answered.

"Yep," I agreed. "Seven thousand and thirty-eight seems about right."

The passengers' clothing was brown and wrinkled. They looked exhausted, yet they smiled and laughed. I knew how they felt. They were finally in America.

And then I saw her. "Mama!" I called out. Mama's face was wrapped in a faded tichel. In her arms, she clutched a little girl. Luba was much taller than when I had left Kolno. The look in her eyes was more intelligent than I remembered, but her curly hair still sprung out in all directions. Did her cheeks still dimple when she smiled? Did she remember her older sister? Our eyes locked. A little smile played on Luba's face. Her dimples deepened, and she giggled.

"Luba!" I shouted. My baby sister remembered me!

Mama gazed into my eyes. "Toba, how much you've grown!" She held me at arm's length, staring.

Did she notice my starched dress? Did she see that I had mended my own tights, that I had ironed Velvel's shirt?

Mama wrapped her arms around me. She held me and smoothed my hair.

"What a young lady my Toba has become!"

I glanced at Papa. Tears ran down into his thick beard. "Pesya! Luba!" he whispered. He grabbed Luba and swung her around in a circle. Mama pulled Velvel into a hug. We were all together again.

This was a moment that needed to be captured. Quickly, I took out the paintbrush in my mind and painted my family tangled in a bundle of love. This is how I wanted to remember us, always.

# Historical Note

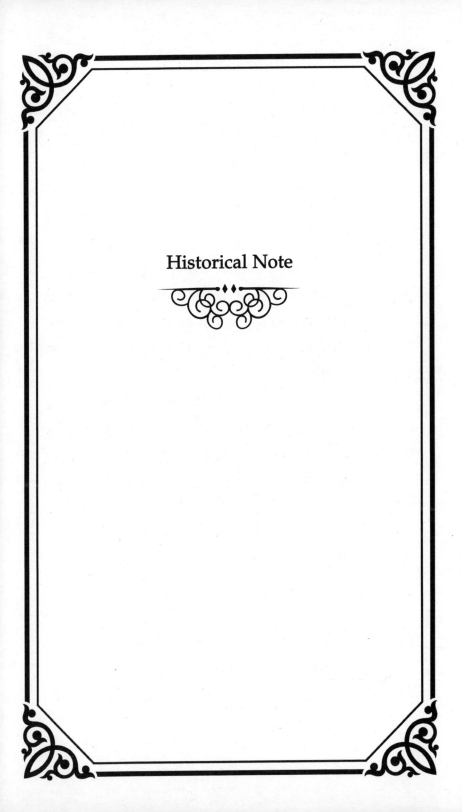

Jewish people in nineteenth century Eastern Europe lived a difficult life. Jews were not allowed to own land or become farmers. Because of this, most made their living buying and selling farm products, such as wool, vegetables, and wheat.

Other Jews became craftsmen, butchers, bakers, goldsmiths or bookbinders. Just like Toba's family, most Jews were very poor, and the non-Jewish peasants around them were poor as well.

In the shtetl, the most prized possession of every Jew was Torah. Men who were able to, learned it day and night and taught it to their sons. Mothers taught Torah to their daughters in the form of practical mitzvos like kashering chickens or taking challah.

Although most of the surrounding villagers were unable to read, many Jewish boys were able to read the alef-beis by the age of five or six.

At the time in history when this story takes place, the ruler of Poland and Russia was Czar Alexander II (the Second). After he was killed, the peasants were very unhappy. In order to distract the peasants from their problems, the new czar, Alexander III (the Third), encouraged the peasants to gang up on the Jewish villagers in raids called pogroms.

With the government's approval, mobs of angry peasants would burn houses, steal animals and household goods, attack and terrify the local Jews. In order to escape the pogroms, thousands of Jews flocked to America, especially between 1886 and 1906.

Because the Jews were so poor, often one family member would go to America to earn money to buy tickets for the rest. Of course, they could barely scrape together enough money for the very cheapest tickets. That meant a miserable trip in the lowest level of the ship, called steerage.

Steerage lacked fresh air, proper beds, or any privacy. It was noisy and dirty, with many passengers feeling ill and weak during their two week voyage. Many elderly people remained behind in the shtetl because the journey would have been too difficult for them.

When the immigrants entered America, they were filled with joy, for they knew that they would be safe from pogroms. However, there were still many obstacles to overcome.

Americans did not want new diseases brought into their land. When the immigrants reached Ellis Island, like Toba, they each had to be checked for illness. Many sick immigrants were sent back to their home countries.

Unable to pronounce foreign names correctly, and in the interest of helping newcomers become more American, officials at Ellis Island often shortened or altered last names. The author's own family experienced this: "Czapelski" became "Shapell" when they came from Poland.

Poor immigrants couldn't afford to live anywhere but in small, overcrowded tenement apartments in American cities.

People slept wherever there was space. Some of these buildings had no light, running water, or heating in the winter. It was hard for Jews to get jobs, because all of the factories operated on Shabbos.

Like Papa, some Jews worked in their homes so they could still keep Shabbos, and worked at night and on Sundays instead.

The Jewish People experienced many hardships through every century of history. Our emunah in Hashem and our love of Torah and mitzvos have kept us strong and united.

Today, it is easy to things for granted, like running water, washing machines, and the freedom not to work on Shabbos.

When we learn about the challenges of our ancestors, we can take inspiration from their strength  and use it to meet the challenges we face today.

# Glossary

**Ah gutten tug** - Yiddish for "Good day"

**Aibishter** - Yiddish for "the One above;" G-d

**Aleph-Beis** - Hebrew alphabet

**Beis Hamikdosh** - Holy Temple

**Bekesheh** - Traditional long coat

**Bentch(ing)** - Verb meaning to bless;
Noun referring to the Grace after Meals

**Boruch Hashem** - Thank G-d

**Boychick** - Yiddish for "little boy"

**Brocha** - (Noun) Blessing

**Challah** - Sabbath loaves

**Chosson** - Bridegroom, betrothed

**Czar** - Emperor or king; ruler of Russia

**Gemara** - The Talmud

**Hashem** - G-d

**Hu-aitz** - Yiddish pronunciation of the
blessing over fruit, Ha-etz

**Im Yirtzeh Hashem** - G-d willing

**Kallah** - Bride, betrothed

**Kinderlach** - Yiddish for "little children"

**Melamed** - School teacher

**Mezuzah** - Parchment scroll inscribed with handwritten text of
the Shema and affixed to the doorpost of every
Jewish home or building

**Mitzvah** - One of the 613 commandments of the Torah;
good deed

**Modeh Ani** - Prayer of gratitude recited immediately
upon awakening

**Negel Vasser** - Ritual handwashing

**Oy (vey)** - Yiddish expression of dismay

**Peyos** - Sidelocks, left uncut as a mitzvah

**Pogrom** - A publicly sanctioned violent attack
    specifically targeting Jews

**Reb** - Respectful title for an adult male

**Sefer, Seforim** - Book(s)

**Shabbos** - Sabbath

**Shehakol** - Blessing made on various foods

**Shema** - The "Hear 'O Israel" Prayer

**Shmatteh** - Yiddish for "rag"

**Shtetl** - Village

**Shul** - Synagogue

**Siddur, Siddurim** - Prayer book(s)

**Talmid Chochom** - Torah scholar

**Tefillas Haderech** - Prayer for a safe trip

**Tehillim** - Psalms

**Torah** - The Five Books of Moses; also refers to the entire
    body of Jewish wisdom, laws and teaching

**Tzedoka** - Charity

**Tzitzis** - Four-cornered garments with strings,
    worn by Jewish males

**Yarmulka** - Headcovering worn by men and boys, kippah

**Yid, Yidden** - Yiddish for "Jew(s)"

**Zeeseh Maydeleh** - Yiddish for "sweet little girl"

**Zeeskeit** - Yiddish for "sweet one"

**Zeide** - Grandfather

# BOOKS IN THE

Israel in the days of
Kind Chizkiyahu

Spain • 1492

Eastern Europe1800's

Russia • 1853

North Dakota • 1897

New York • 1905

WWI • Poland • 1914

WWII • Hungary • 1944

America • present day

# MAKING JEWISH HISTORY FUN TO READ!